THE SIXTH SENSE
AND OTHER STORIES

THE SIXTH SENSE

AND OTHER STORIES

by

Jessie Haas

Greenwillow Books, New York

The quotation at the beginning of "The Sixth Sense"
comes from *Horsemanship,* by Waldemar Seunig
(New York: Doubleday & Co., 1956).
Though it didn't suit James's mood on that
particular day, it is an excellent book,
recommended to all serious riders.

Library of Congress Cataloging-in-Publication Data
Haas, Jessie.
The sixth sense and other stories.
Summary: A collection of interconnected short
stories exploring the relationships of people
to each other and to the animals in their lives.
[1. Interpersonal relations—Fiction.
2. Animals—Fiction]   I. Title.
PZ7.H1129Si 1988   [Fic]   88-45226
ISBN 0-688-08129-0

To my parents,
with love and thanks

And thanks also to
Eileen Martin
and
Christina Major

CONTENTS

THE SIXTH SENSE
AND OTHER STORIES

THE
WAKE

I FIRST KNEW something was wrong by the quiet. The little
brown yard within the picket fence was bare, silent, empty.

That wasn't unusual for an early spring afternoon. It was
slightly too cool for a cat to sun in comfort, and Aunt Mil
herself was usually indoors, even on a warmer day. She
would have heard the school bus stop at the corner, and she
would be putting on the kettle, taking the gingersnaps out of
the oven.

No scent of gingersnaps today, though. The kitchen windows looked blank and dark. Worry began to nip at me. Aunt
Mil is old, older than my grandmother would be if she still

lived. Anything could happen, and not just old age; burglars, or murderers, even . . .

"Use your imagination for something worthwhile!" Aunt Mil would snap, hearing any of this. I went boldly up the flagstone walk. The first crocuses were in bud, their yellow and purple heads piercing last year's brown leaves like arrows shot from underground. Today's job would be raking out the bulb beds.

As I opened the kitchen door I thought, Maybe she's gone somewhere. The house behind the door seemed silent and empty, dark, and too cool.

"Aunt Mil?"

Sun streamed in the window over the sink, across the white-fuzzed cactus plants and colorful nylon pot scrubbers. "Aunt Mil?" I put my knapsack on the clean table and went toward the living room door, letting alarm in again. Oh, God, what if . . .

My heart gave a great frightened thump when I saw her. The house was so still and dim, I was sure it was empty. But Aunt Mil sat in her armchair before me, bolt upright; alive. I saw that at once.

Then I saw the tears, burning and carving down her face like silver acid. She sat utterly motionless, but the tears ran and dripped off her grim, straight jaw. They rooted me in my tracks. Aunt Mil, *crying*?

But when I looked in her lap, I knew. Curled there, fluffy and frail, was her ancient cat, Puttins, and he was much stiller than Aunt Mil.

The breath rushed out of me in a strange relief, and I started to go to her. Halfway across the rug, I began to feel like a fool. I felt awkward and miserable, and my foolish face smiled. Weird, hysterical laughter fluttered at my stomach.

The Wake

"Oh, Aunt Mil!" I put one arm around her stiff shoulders. They didn't relax. If anything, they seemed to push me away.

"Oh, Aunt Mil!" I said again. I dropped on my knees beside the chair and reached over the arm for her hand. Her hands curled around the old cat's body, and I touched him. He was cold and unyielding, like a piece of wood covered with fur. She must have been sitting there with him a long time. I clasped her hand tightly. It was cool and slack.

Talk. Break through. "When did it happen?" I asked, and in the ensuing silence I heard how my harsh voice startled the house. Aunt Mil made no response beyond a slow, unseeing shake of the head.

I drew back to look at her. She seemed fierce, with her grim jaw and gash of a mouth, the bright, burning eyes that had never gotten old. She looked indomitable. She looked every inch the tough old battle-ax I'd always known. But . . .

"Aunt Mil?"

Okay, this was one for a grown-up. "I'm calling Mum," I said, and I got up and went out to the sunny kitchen. The telephone receiver was warm, the old-fashioned dial stiff and loud.

The phone rang five times. I'll let it go ten, I thought, but on number six Mum picked it up.

"Hello?" she said breathlessly. She would have been outdoors, looking at the new green tips of her own bulbs.

"Mum? It's me. Uh—can you come over?"

"What's wrong?"

"Aunt Mil—" For a second my voice squeezed off. Say it! I commanded, knowing the thoughts that would race through my mother's mind. "Her . . . her cat is dead, and . . . she's just sitting there. She won't answer me."

3

"I'll be right over," said my mother, and crashed down the receiver.

I hung up more slowly, relieved and dissatisfied. Mum would be here in ten minutes. She'd know what to do.

But *I* was Aunt Mil's special relative. *I* was the one she liked best, the one who understood her. I was the one who knew poor old Puttins. I couldn't say his name to Mum and rely on her to recognize it. How could *Mum* comfort Aunt Mil?

I heard a tearing sniff from the living room and remembered how even the most silent, unsobbing tears bring a runny nose. I picked up the box of tissues from its spot on the clean counter and went back to the living room.

The way she snatched the tissue, I knew it gave more comfort than my hug had. She dried her face before she blew her nose. I remembered the last time I cried, how the tears itched and burned like some chemical running down my face. Aunt Mil dropped the tissue on the brown rug and reached for another.

"Mum's coming right over."

She didn't look at me. She was staring straight ahead. New tears came up in her eyes and started down her cheeks. She lifted the tissue to blot them, but opened it wide instead and buried her whole face, shaking silently.

I sat in the other chair and looked off out the window, embarrassed and feeling stupid. I thought of Gram's funeral, three years ago, when I was twelve. Though Gram was her little sister, the last family member of her generation, Aunt Mil stood straight as an arrow, unshaken. Mum and my uncles clung to her, and she supported them all. Now she was shattered by the loss of a moth-eaten old cat, whom we'd known was going to die soon, anyway. . . .

The Wake

I come two afternoons a week for house- and yardwork, and all winter I'd helped Aunt Mil fight for him. He needed special food, which he didn't like, and we were always dreaming up ways to make it tasty and to keep him clean, free of fleas and free of colds. "If he can just make it through till spring . . ." she said. The most we hoped for was one last summer, a final season of sun in the garden, and a final subdued rapture in the catnip bed.

But we still lost, even after all that trying. So hard to believe that this was not just a temporary setback.

I sneaked a look at him, in Aunt Mil's lap. How could it be that if I touched him now, he would not raise his head with a rusty trill? How could it be that he was no longer the cat we used to know?

His soul is fled, I thought experimentally, and because he wasn't *my* cat, because I was pushed away by Aunt Mil's solitary grief, I found I was excited. That sounds terrible, but since the shiny coffin that held Gram was lowered into the hole, I've been wondering about death. Now here it was, and how simple! How utterly strange!

Outside, a car ripped through an early-spring puddle, stopped quickly and noisily outside the picket fence. Aunt Mil's eyes shifted around the room, and she curled her hands closer to the body of the cat. I wondered, in the remaining minute of silence, if I'd done the right thing.

Then the kitchen door opened, and Mum poured in; comfortably round, puffing a little as she struggled out of her heavy, camel-colored coat and straightened her clothes, bustling and rustling through the doorway. Aunt Mil put her chin up a quarter of an inch higher, and her mouth tightened in its downward curve. She glared at my poor bewildered mother for a minute. Then a fresh flood of tears; her face crumpled and she bent her head, pressing one hand across her eyes.

"Aunty Mil?"

It would have been better if Mum didn't sound so shocked. But she rushed over and hugged Aunt Mil into her bosom. Aunt Mil collapsed there and wept loudly, with harsh, groaning sobs. My face heated. I went to look out the window at the backyard.

Like the front, it was bare and brown; neat from our work last fall, but bleak. All that showed to foretell summer's gorgeous perennial border was a row of straw-colored stubble along the fence and the big compost pile, where all organic refuse underwent its miraculous transformation. A patch of dingy snow lingered under the forsythia, which showed as yet no sign of bloom.

As I looked, wishing I dared put my fingers in my ears, I saw Aunt Mil's younger cat, Robert, squeeze through the pickets and tiptoe across the muddy yard. I went to the back door to let him in.

Robert arched his back in pleased surprise and stroked himself against my leg, giving me a direct, sentimental look from his yellow eyes. I scooped him up to hug. "Oh, Robert!" He was warm and sleek, vibrating with purrs and struggling with all his muscular strength to get free. He hadn't *asked* to be picked up—hadn't I noticed? But I hugged him a moment against his will, holding him like a poultice against the unexpected hurt in my heart. Poor old Putts!

Robert squirmed free and dropped to the floor with a heavy thud, still purring. I went back toward the living room. He followed slowly at first, then galloped ahead and dashed dramatically into the middle of the rug.

Aunt Mil was sitting up straight again, blowing her nose.

The Wake

Mum perched on the arm of the chair, one plump, warm arm around Aunt Mil's shoulders.

"Kris can do it," she was saying, "if you have a shovel."

Oh, *God*, Mum!

Aunt Mil brought the blasted tissue down from her face and saw Robert taking his buccaneer stance in the center of the rug. *More* tears—where are they coming from?—poured down her cheeks. She bent forward over the dead cat in her lap and snapped her fingers.

Like a buccaneer deciding it might not be a trap, Robert swaggered over, keeping one eye on Mum. He rubbed his chin hard, once, on Aunt Mil's fingers. Then his yellow eyes flashed beyond, to the cat in her lap.

There had existed between Puttins and Robert a kind of armed neutrality, tested from time to time. Each was jealous of the other. If Robert was playing with a piece of string and Puttins tapped it, even once, then no amount of coaxing would lure Robert back to the game for at least twenty minutes. They never shared a lap, so unless I was there, one of them would always be curled in a chair across the room from Aunt Mil, giving her the cold shoulder. Usually it was Robert.

Now, when his hot yellow glare found Puttins, I expected him to turn away in an ostentatious miff. Instead, he stood where he was, lifting his nose in tiny bobbing motions to test the scent. He knows, I thought. Aunt Mil's eyes dried as she watched him, and even Mum saw something going on, and was silent.

Robert minced forward. Aunt Mil leaned slowly back, so that the old cat showed plainly on her lap. When he was close, Robert reared on his hind legs, placing one paw delicately and weightlessly on Aunt Mil's thigh for balance. He stretched his neck to its utmost limit and smelled the tips of Puttins's dull old hairs, bobbing his nose along them. His eyes glared beyond, into space. His ears were wild.

At the end of this long moment he sank slowly down to a sitting position and stayed there, thinking. We all watched him, still, as if we awaited some pronouncement. Eventually Robert stalked a little way off and lay down, ears back; *definitely* thinking. What he thought would never be revealed, and I think we all sighed.

In the silence Mum sighed again, looking at the four of us: old aunt, teenage daughter, dead cat, live cat. How was she going to tidy all this up and get home in time to make supper?

"Aunty Mil," she asked at last, hesitantly. "What do you want?"

Aunt Mil's face twisted for a second. What a stupid thing to ask, I thought. She wants him *back*!

Mum went on. "We can . . . bury him now, if you want, Kris and I. Or if you'd rather wait, I'll take you home to supper with me."

The expediency, mingled with her kindness, made me ashamed—but at least she was doing something, taking charge. Maybe I did understand Aunt Mil a little better, but I was useless.

Watching Robert, Aunt Mil had gone quite a way back toward normal, so I wasn't surprised when she finally spoke. "Thank you, Grace, but I'll do it myself. Later. I'll come to dinner with you now."

At home, Mum went to work in the kitchen, and Aunt Mil helped, slicing vegetables and setting the table. Outwardly she seemed all right, but I felt her quiet and saw how she was bowed down, darkened and diminished. Mum chattered; Aunt Mil answered. Feeling superfluous, I went to my room to do homework. Homework, on a Friday afternoon!

When supper preparations were over, I heard the television come on. Time for Mum's favorite game show. Aunt Mil was plunked down on the couch to watch too. She despises game shows. Mum doesn't know this, of course. Amiably she was trying to amuse and distract Aunt Mil, feeling it was the right thing to do.

Should I go down and rescue her? Bring her up to my room for a little rational conversation? That's what she says when we bump into each other at a gathering of relatives. *"Now, for a little rational conversation!"*

But before, when we had rational conversation, it was about books and old movies, compost, plant propagation, and interspecies relations. Before, I had never seen Aunt Mil shattered, nor heard her sob. I stayed where I was, doing math problems that all came out wrong.

Greg and Amy came home on the late bus, full of news. Supper started to smell good. Then Dad came home. The house changed from a relaxed, boring place to a boring place humming with Standards, Expectations, and Responsibilities.

"What are you doing, Kris?" he asked outside my door.

"Math."

"Good!" He was surprised. On the other side of the wall beside my desk, I heard Amy give an irritated *tsk*. She was only changing. Dad said she spent too much time on her appearance. True enough, actually.

Mum came rustling and puffing up the stairs, following Dad into their bedroom. I decided to go down and be with

Aunt Mil and stepped out into the hall where I could hear everything.

". . . never seen her go to pieces like that. She seems all right now, but she *cried* so, Steve!"

Dad made a noise that might have been concerned and sympathetic. Then he said, "Foolish to waste all that emotional energy on an animal!"

"They're all she has!"

"Why doesn't she go to the Senior Center, or spend time with the family?"

"Shh, Steve!"

"Well, it's *silly!*"

"Yes, I know. I thought I'd send Kris to spend the night with her."

Their footsteps were starting to leave the room. I closed my door sharply and headed downstairs.

Spend the night?

Normally I love to, because face it, Aunt Mil is my best friend. We drink a lot of tea and eat cookies, crackers and cheese, or popcorn. We have rational conversations or find a Leslie Howard movie on late, late TV. We make laps for the cats.

She still sat on the couch, apparently watching the news. I sat, too, facing halfway between her and the TV, ready to be there if she spoke.

She neither spoke nor looked. She kept her straight, unwinking gaze on the television set, even through commercials. By not one gesture did she acknowledge our special kinship.

I looked down at my empty lap. I wish *I* had a cat. We have no animals in our house, except a pair of goldfish that serve a decorative function. That's why our house is so boring.

The Wake

I think people *need* animals, and I have some theories why. The middle part of our brain, the one that handles emotions, is the same structure shared by all mammals; we've just added something more. Therefore I think we understand all mammals—or would if we would allow ourselves. To see an animal is to see an inner part of us, before it was hidden and hampered by our intellect. Little kids love animals, and fairy tales are full of them. Also, they're more beautiful than us. When you consider all this, and you consider how boring this house is, with only people and goldfish, then you have to consider that my father is wrong.

Wrong or not, he now came brisk and hearty into the room and went to the bar to mix himself a drink. While he did, he talked cheerfully to Aunt Mil about a wonderful seventy-year-old man he'd met last week, who went to the Senior Center every day and had a tremendous lot of fun playing Bingo. The corner of Aunt Mil's mouth compressed in a bitter smile. She asked him to mix her a drink, too, and he did, looking surprised.

It was a clear, cold gin and tonic. Watching the thirsty way she gulped it, I was reminded that alcohol is a drug. Aunt Mil doesn't take it often. "I'm hoarding the few brain cells I have left to me," she likes to say. She also says that alcohol is a depressant, so why she was drinking it now, I didn't know.

When we'd watched the newscast right through to sports and weather, it was time to eat. Over supper, we heard what Greg and Amy did in school—again. We heard a little of what Mum did in school, where she teaches the morning kindergarten class. We heard a lot about what Dad did in school, where he teaches high-school chemistry. I have to take his class next year, and frankly I don't look forward to it.

11

THE SIXTH SENSE

We heard nothing of Aunt Mil's cat, companion of fifteen years, dying in her lap that very afternoon.

Aunt Mil had a poor appetite. Mum kept coaxing her to eat, as if that would solve something. Dad tried to draw her out on subjects like Motivating Students in the Sciences, and The Graying of America. She made him short answers which ended with periods. She had great, if searing, things to think about, and all this chatter kept her from them.

Supper was done. Dishes were washed. Over coffee, after a decent interval, Aunt Mil asked to go home.

Mum fluttered and protested, clearly showing that she thought it a morbid impulse. "At least take Kris," she said. "You shouldn't be alone."

Aunt Mil's eyes swung to look at me. They were tired but personal. They saw *me*, not a commodity to ward off loneliness.

"Does Kris want to come?"

I could only nod. I did and I didn't. She nodded too. She did and didn't want to have me.

I packed nightgown, toothbrush, and the book I was reading—*The Ring of Solomon* by Konrad Lorenz—in a shopping bag. I also packed homework, because it would look good, and I might even do some. We drove to Aunt Mil's dark house.

Mum shone the headlights up the walk as Aunt Mil went ahead to turn on the yard light. As soon as she was out of the car, Mum said, "Thank you for doing this, Kris."

"Mm." I was doing it for Aunt Mil, not for Mum. I wasn't all that willing.

"I worry about her, living all alone. It must be hard to stay rational."

"Mm."

The Wake

"We'll be at the hockey finals in White River tomorrow morning, but we should be back by one. Call when you want a ride home."

"I might walk," I said. The yard light came on, and I got out of the car. " 'Night, Mum."

As I closed the door I remembered for some reason the time when I would never say good night or goodbye to Mum and Dad. It was always, "See you in the morning," and I thought if I didn't say it, I might not see them. They might stop breathing in the night, or go away. If I ever forgot, I would have to trek down to the bathroom, blinking and pretending to have been asleep, in order to complete the ritual. They had to hear me too. It was a pact.

I opened the car door again, as I thought it hadn't closed right, and before slamming it I said, "See you tomorrow."

When I got inside, Aunt Mil was no longer in the kitchen. She stood in the bedroom doorway with her coat on, looking in. That must be where she laid him, on her bed or on the chair.

I went up to the guest room, carefully stepping on the carpeted middles of the stairs. The door squeaked, so I slid through the opening as soon as it was wide enough and left it open. I put my bag softly on the table and sat on the bed, not jouncing the springs.

It was the guest room, but the books in the case were mine; scroungings from secondhand bookstores, and more expensive ones, gifts from Aunt Mil. The theme—animal behavior; the relation between human and animal, the animal in human, and the human in animal. Serious books and silly books, side by side in rows. My father doesn't know about them, and he won't, until someday he'll see them all gathered in my college room, and he'll ask if I've picked my major.

Aunt Mil's guest room, then, is really *my* room, where I may be truly alone, free of questions at the door and tsking from the other side of the wall, where I may do my real studying and not just my homework. But tonight the silence came in the open door, possessing, making the place as strange as a motel room. I sat still and listened.

After a while I heard Aunt Mil's closet door open and shut. Nothing more. Half an hour went by on the bedside alarm clock. I thought, I'm not here just to sit in my room. So I went down again, treading in the middle of the stairs. To Aunt Mil's room.

She was bending over the bed in her straight way, folding only at the hips and tucking a very old plaid bathrobe around something small: Puttins. So I had touched his fur for the last time.

She looked up as I came in, meeting my eyes honestly. Her eyes said to mine, I have to do this by myself. You understand. Then she said, "Kris, you could help me. Will you go out to the porch and find a box?"

I could see why she wouldn't want to do that. On the porch were boxes that presents and groceries had come in, waiting to take presents out or to transport dug-up plants or books. They said WHISKEY on the sides, or VERMONT CHEESE, or TOMATOES. Which would be a suitable coffin for a good old cat?

The cheese box seemed the right size. It said VERMONT CHEESE on all four sides and the top. I thought of covering it with brown paper so Aunt Mil wouldn't have to see, but that would take ages.

She didn't seem to notice. She opened the box on the bed,

14

then tenderly lifted old Putts in the bathrobe and laid him in it. For a second I saw a puff of fur and knew it as one of the long tufts of his pantaloons. Then Aunt Mil closed the box with quiet, final hands and picked it up. She looked around for a spot to put it, seeming almost helpless, and set it down at last on the bureau.

Now, for the first time I spotted Robert, lying between the pillows of the double bed. He was curled up as if asleep, but his eyes were open, clear and yellow, watching us. He looked like a wild animal. Usually when I look at an animal, I think of the similarities between us, but then I was reminded of the differences.

Meanwhile, Aunt Mil stood looking at the box, her mouth stretched long, like the beginning of crying and like a smile. When she felt me looking, though, her face softened. She said, "How about a cup of tea?"

She made Earl Grey tea, handling all the implements as if they were heavy. She paused often in the midst of doing things, looking down at her hands. Then she would push on.

While the tea steeped she got a tray and set out the cups, cream, and honey. No gingersnaps. When the color was right, she dumped the tea leaves into the bag beneath the sink, for the compost pile. She rinsed the basket, put it in the drainer, and took the tray into the living room.

The living room was where her husband died, so long ago that most people think of her as an old maid. Now Putts had died there, and I wondered what she thought of that. Maybe it should be called the dying room.

I took my usual chair, and she took hers. At this point Robert and old Putts would generally arrive, select laps, and inspect the viands. I watched nervously for Robert; it would be bad if he came in and chose me, leaving Aunt Mil's lap empty. But for whatever reason, Robert stayed where he was between the pillows of the double bed.

Aunt Mil poured the fragrant tea. We added our milk and honey, with the silence gathering thickly around us. Aunt Mil stared straight ahead, sipping slowly. One good thing: I could see the tea was a satisfaction to her.

In the absolute stillness I could tell by the change in her breathing that she was about to speak. Was it a speaking that would have come earlier, if I hadn't panicked and called for Mum?

"He came to get me, Kris," she said at last. She gave me a proud look. "He knew—I believe he knew—and he came for me." Her mouth twisted in a terrifying expression, a smile of grief and great love. "That's not a bad last gift, is it?"

Tears had started to pour again. She reached for the tissues. Muffled in one, she said, "Sorry, Kris. If this is too much for you, go home. It's all right."

Yes, I wanted to go home. I was covered with guilt, to see Aunt Mil consider me in the midst of her pain. But I shook my head, which she didn't see, and sipped my perfumed tea, hoping it might warm and loosen the cold, tight spot within. I knew I must respond, before this was over, or nothing would ever be the same.

Then I heard my voice ask, "What was it like?" and I could have slain myself.

Aunt Mil looked up, as startled as I, and after a moment gave a slow, considering nod. "Yes," she said. "It was peaceful, and . . . terrible. He curled on my lap and seemed to sleep. Then I saw he wasn't breathing. I thought he'd already died, but his ribs moved again, after a while . . . a harsh breath. I thought it was the last, but it went on. The breaths were so far apart that each one startled me. After a while, no more came. That's all."

I was trembling and couldn't stop. I got up and poured another cup of tea, drank it straight down, hot and plain. Aunt Mil watched me.

"Brandy's the thing for us," she said. "You know where it is, Kris, in the cupboard by the telephone. Get two shot glasses."

The brandy bottle has always been there, going down by slow inches over the years. The shot glasses are most often used as vases for tiny flowers; johnny-jump-ups, or forget-me-nots. I set them on the tray, and Aunt Mil poured them full.

"Alcohol's a depressant," I said.

"It warms you." Aunt Mil raised the glass to eye level, turning it a little in the light. "Let's drink to . . . the Old Boy, wherever he is."

She drained the glass. They were big, man-sized shot glasses that used to belong to her husband, Kenny. I sipped and felt the brandy burn a thin trail down my esophagus. I waited, half expecting Aunt Mil to hurl the glass; not into the fireplace, for there is none. The wall? The TV set? No, her hand clenched around it, as if she would crush it in her fist.

"You don't get in practice, Kris," she said. "I used to think you would. I thought that making it through one death would prepare you for the next. It doesn't. They just pile up."

Oh?

She poured herself another shot of brandy and drank it down. I began to feel alarmed.

"Death is part of life. That's what people say, to sound

wise. But what does that do for *me*, Kris? How does that give me back my old cat, who loved me? Hmm?"

Nothing can do that, I could have said, but that would only be sounding wise. I sipped my brandy and looked, my eyes smarting from the fumes, at Aunt Mil's angry, bleak face.

"You never cried when Gram died. That's what Mum says, anyway. . . ."

"I didn't. She knew what she was doing."

She knew what she was doing? In Gram I remember a person softer than Aunt Mil, sweeter, yet much more distant. Like Mum, she hid herself deep in a cushiony layer of domesticity. She was a diabetic; I forget how she died.

"What do you mean?"

She took a moment to reply. "She'd been sick long enough to come to terms with it. I believe she did—*I* did. I thought she was lucky. She was spared a lot of suffering."

"And—" But I lacked the courage to ask my question. Instead, I poured out a cup of tea. Last one; time to make another pot.

"When Kenny died," said Aunt Mil with a kind of relentless understanding, "we were sitting here in these chairs, reading. When I heard the little sound, I finished my sentence and looked up. I saw at once that he was dead. I *recognized* that moment, Kris. Kenny was always well; I had never dreamed of anything like that, but as I looked at him, I felt I'd always known it was coming, just that way."

Telling this story, her face got leaner and harder, as if her courage rose up in her at the memory of past trials. "It was a terrible time. I wanted to die too. But I remembered that feeling, and sometimes I've taken comfort in it; as if it had been planned, so it was all right."

Her bright, proud eyes challenged me to call that silly; then they softened, as she saw me again, clutching my cup, shaking all over.

"This is too much for you. I'll call your mother." She started to rise.

"No!"

She sank back slowly, incompletely. "You're sure? If you stay, I won't stop talking. Or . . . you could go to bed."

"Not till you do." I could say that without unclenching my teeth.

"No," she said. "This is the wake."

The other wake I've been to was my grandmother's. I remember her in the shiny coffin, looking like a statue carved in wax. I remember the relatives coming into the room that smelled fake-sweet, with thin, canned music playing. They were dressed with dark elegance and looked nervous. They went up to the coffin. Many flushed and burst into tears. They went to squeeze the hands of my mother, uncles, and Aunt Mil. Then they came out where the folding chairs were set in rows. Sometimes they sat by themselves a minute and tried to stop crying. Sometimes their eyes were already dry, and combing the crowd. They formed little chatting groups and had a good time.

For Puttins' wake we would stay up all night, drinking as much tea as was required, and remembering. "It's what I dread most," said Aunt Mil, "the forgetting that happens when you leave someone behind and you go on." The wake was a way of staving that off, of loving, and fixing in the memory against the day when one could not remember how the lost one looked, or the sound of his voice. At first light we would take the old cat out and bury him in the garden.

"I thought we'd put him in the catnip bed," said Aunt Mil. "Remember how he'd go straight to it every time you let him out the door?"

That called up a vivid image of the old boy pottering across the lawn, slow and a little wobbly, but sure of his goal. By the time I knew him, he was past kittenish antics, even under the influence of the Drug, but he would sit in the sun beside the catnip plants, eyes narrowed to golden slits, purring at the whole world. I smiled, remembering. Aunt Mil was smiling too.

"When he was younger, he used to come wake me in the morning, try to open my eyes and mouth with his paw." She laughed. "I remember how shocked and repulsed he was when I brought Robert home. For months, whenever things went wrong or he didn't get his way, he'd go over and cuff the kitten."

"Will you get another kitten?"

"I don't know, Kris. I've been debating for months—I don't believe I have another whole cat-life left to me. But I've always had two, and I think it's better. Easier to remember that they're *cats*, and not make stunted children of them."

"Dad thinks you do that already, because you never had kids."

Aunt Mil's eyes flashed angrily.

"Dad's a poop," I said.

She sighed, weighing her responsibility. Should she reprimand me for this unfilial remark, or agree?

"I know the difference," she said. "I think . . . it matters less than people like your father can imagine."

"Dad thinks animals are things, like chairs."

"When you raise an animal," said Aunt Mil, pursuing her own line of thought, "it progresses only to a certain point.

You don't get intellectual companionship. You get something else, which is beautiful and important. Of course, it isn't enough. But intellect is also not enough."

"People need animals," I said. "The emotional center of our brain is a mammal's brain. We understand them, and they understand us."

"Yes. We love them. I value that old cat more than most humans of my acquaintance. More than many members of my family. Your father would think that downright insane."

"You can't help what you love."

"Nor should you, Kris."

"Did you love Putts more than you loved my grandmother? Is that why you cried?"

For a moment I thought I'd gone too far. Aunt Mil fixed her bright, enigmatic eyes on me and said nothing. I was beginning to flounder for words to cover up this gaffe when she finally said, "Now, that, Kris, is an interesting question."

I waited.

"I loved him more completely," she said, thinking it out, "because there was—I *think*—less of him to know. There wasn't the moral ambiguity. I didn't project onto him my human needs, and so I didn't carry around any history of hurt. Since he was only a cat, I could love every bit of him. Maybe that's how we *should* love people, but I'm not large enough yet."

"Only human," I said, not knowing what I meant.

"Yes. And I cried—I am grieving and angry and frightened—because I have lost the company of someone I love, and I don't know if I'll ever see him again."

I gaped.

"Oh, yes, that's what I said. They claim—these people who've been resuscitated, whom they write the books about—that they were greeted by people they loved, who were dead. Well, that's old, Kris. That was in the folklore *long* before these doctors decided it was okay to notice. I believe, most of the time, that I'll see Kenny again. But . . . I've never read where any of these people mention animals. And I don't know. I just don't know."

Her words fell softly into the pool of silence, and the ripples spread, fainter and fainter. I thought of the dead cat, in the cheese box on the bureau, and the live cat, asleep between the pillows. And us. Poor us. We must die, and everyone we love must die, and we know nothing about it. We can't know. How can we possibly go on living when we can't *know* anything?

On the other hand, what's the alternative?

I found Aunt Mil's eyes on me, kindly. Barring accident, Aunt Mil is going to know the answers a lot sooner than I will. She has lived with the questions for over eighty years, survived many deaths, and she is brave enough to be kind to me while thinking of her old cat. . . .

"Maybe none of those people loved an animal enough to have it come greet them when they died," I said roughly.

"Maybe. That's what I tell myself, and looking around, it seems likely."

We heard a thump from the bedroom, the soft, heavy, concentrated sound of a cat jumping down from someplace high. We looked toward the doorway. In a few seconds Robert came strolling through. He paused, blinking at us like a movie star vamping the adoring throngs, then displayed himself in an elegant, ostentatious stretch. He came over, rubbed his chin briefly on Aunt Mil's fingers, and went to the kitchen to check out the food dish.

22

The Wake

New tears ran slowly down Aunt Mil's face. She was smiling, too, mouth stretching. I got up, crossed the little space between us, and hugged her straight, thin, hard, old shoulders. She sniffed loudly.

"Put the kettle on, Kris. We'll have another pot of tea."

HORSE
MAN

THE GIRL on the brown horse saluted and left the ring on a long rein. The judge, seated in a horse trailer parked at the end of the ring, spoke briefly to her scribe. Beyond the yellow rope, the spectators looked toward the entrance for the next competitor.

But the sand stretched empty. Blue paper covers of programs flashed in the sun as two dozen people opened them at once, turning to page six.

The next rider should be number twenty-eight, James Mac-Liesh. Horse, Ghazal. Owner, MacLiesh Farm. Time of Test, ten-fifteen.

It's ten-fifteen now.

Horse Man

The scribe shuffled through her papers, then rose from her lawn chair and came down the ramp. There were no loudspeakers. Arenas were widely spaced throughout the meadows, and the emphasis was on concentration.

"Number twenty-eight is scratched," the scribe called. "Is number seventeen ready to go?"

A shirt-sleeved girl doing canter transitions on a fat white mare shouted from the warm-up area, "No, I'm not!"

"Okay, you don't have to go until your time," the scribe assured her. "Would someone be willing to run back to the kitchen and get us a couple of sodas?"

James sighed and turned away. A morbid impulse had brought him to this ring at just this time, and now he regretted it. The white horse made him think of Ghazal—clumsy, stupid Ghazal, who had stepped on himself last week while landing from a jump. He'd torn off a shoe and cut the bulb of his hoof. He needed at least three weeks' rest, and he was scratched from this, the two-day dressage show toward which James had been working since early spring.

Sigh. He looked around for his cousin Gloria, who had come with him today.

When he found her, her back was turned, and she was taking a picture.

James had come because he couldn't stay away, but Gloria was working; photographing riders who might buy the pictures, getting material for the local papers, and taking pictures for herself, to swell her portfolio and sharpen her eye.

There were hundreds of pictures to take: bright polo bandages on the flashing legs of horses; foam spattered on sweat-dark chests; bits and buckles twinkling in the sun, the glow of clean leather; chestnut, black, bay, and silver hides; the precise touch of a blunt chrome spur to a horse's rib; the flick of the wrist deploying the long dressage whip; a jaw yielding softly, a jaw clenched hard; the pricked ears and bright eyes of distraction, the back-turned ears and dreaming, serious eyes of a horse who paid attention. Horses made ugly by their riders, made beautiful by their riders.

James saw, and ached to *be* here. Now he was nothing—a small, insubstantial person walking on the ground. He had no horse to make him important. Nothing to talk about, nothing to do. Acquaintances riding past seemed not to see him, and he didn't bring himself to their attention.

His own sneakers caught his eye. He looked down at them glumly. Sneakers, not boots; symbolic—

The camera was now pointed at him. He jerked up his head in sharp indignation, but too late.

"I'm going to call it 'Grounded,'" said Gloria. "Poor James!"

James gave her a long glare that she didn't see. But he thought, too, of how he must have looked, and after a moment he hoisted his mouth into a near smile and followed the movements of Gloria's camera, alertly if blankly. He would keep his self-pity locked inside from now on, where no one could take pictures of it.

Deliberately, because he had no mental focus of his own today, he made himself think about what she was seeing.

It was people as much as horses. James always saw horses first, but Gloria was seeing, as well, the sleek twelve-year-olds on their multithousand-dollar ponies, and the grubby, earnest twelve-year-olds who had to try ten times as hard, with no expensive teacher to tell them how. She saw the multitude of strong, handsome girls, the horsey beauties James liked so much to look at, and she saw the men, who were fewer. She saw the patient craft in the faces of middle-aged riders, the compensating they had to do, and the knowledge they had exchanged for limberness. And she saw . . .

And she saw the woman.

The woman rode by them on an incredible black warm-blood, bringing him down fluently from his warm-up work. She was *perfect!*

James turned in his tracks as she passed. He saw her halt the horse in two strides beside a man; bending her head to speak to him, sun glowing on her dark French braid . . . what a lovely neck! She wore a sleeveless riding shirt; her arms were bare and brown and beautiful, and she wore gloves, which seemed beautiful too.

"Isn't he amazing?" Gloria murmured. She sounded appropriately awestruck, but the camera clicked away, recording minute variations of the scene.

"Mmm," said James. How peculiar that Gloria, for once, was seeing only the horse! But he hastened to make clear that he, too, was gawking just at horseflesh. "Lotta power in those britches," he said, nodding to the warm-blood's gleaming, muscled haunches.

Gloria gasped. He glanced at her. The camera drifted down from her eye, and she stared at him, openmouthed and blushing. Then she started to laugh.

"James, I was talking about the *man!*"

"*What?*" James looked again and saw with indignation that the man's hand rested on the beautiful woman's knee. He had a strange face; triangular, big-nosed, with shiny, smooth-stretched skin the color of polished mahogany. His long greenish eyes were lifted to hers. They gazed into each other's faces as if nothing on earth would have the power to distract them.

"Man's like catnip, apparently," murmured Gloria. James felt a powerful inner kick of antagonism.

"Ugly as sin!" he said roughly, lifting his eyes to the woman's face. She was instant and glorious refreshment.

"James, stop *gaping*! Come on!" Gloria took him by the arm and towed him a few unresisting steps before he dug in his heels.

"No. I want . . . I want to stay and see these tests."

Gloria let go—perhaps only to snap another picture. Beneath the black box, her mouth smiled. "Okay. I'm going to cruise awhile."

So I'm obvious, thought James. So what! But he made an effort to seem cool, noting his location—Arena Three—where, checking the program, Second Level tests were in progress. He nodded gravely at the program, in case Gloria was still looking, and strolled to a position from which he could watch the woman while appearing to watch the tests.

She looked like a queen, with that beautiful braid for a coronet. She looked like a fairy tale—too lovely to be real. Yet here she was, in the midst of what was to James the most beautiful setting in the world, outshining all. When he could shift his gaze for a few seconds, he saw that her dark, vivid face and glowing eyes drew many glances.

Or *was* it the man? Briefly James wondered if Gloria could be right; what she had heard; who this bozo was. But he had no time to spare for the puzzle. The sight of the woman was doing something wonderful to his spirit, and he didn't want to waste a minute.

When she donned coat and hat and pinned on a number, he checked in the program and found her name—Norah Craig. Norah. Beautiful.

Horse Man

The horse had a Swedish name and belonged to Silver Thimble Farm.

So. Silver Thimble was a coming name, with wealth behind it and a fine herd of the prestigious Swedish warmbloods. It was practically his duty to watch this woman ride; check out the competition.

She was up next, and as she rode away toward the entrance James saw that she was good. She seemed to grow up from the center of the horse's back, like a willow. Her hands were educated and gave back as much as they took. As she trotted around the outside of the ring James watched in fascination the long, gleaming boot, folding softly at the ankle as the dancing foot absorbed concussion.

"Hello, James."

Now someone saw him! He gave the speaker a fleeting glance.

Harriet Marks, who'd bought horses from MacLiesh Farm; an accountant in her fifties; one of the fair to not-so-good riders who made up the lower echelon of the sport, but a great person with whom James always enjoyed a talk. He said hello, and his eyes swung back to Norah and the Swedish horse.

The judge's bell tinkled. Norah proceeded without haste toward the entrance. A perfect arc at the same cadenced trot brought her straight down the center to her halt, with lovely inevitability. She dropped her gloved right hand to her side and bowed her head in salute to the judge. Her grace and grandeur satisfied James deeply.

"Too bad those back legs didn't square," muttered Harriet.

James closed her out of his mind, throwing all his attention into the arena. He made himself judge, rider, and even horse. He executed the first corner in a lovely arc; he felt the power and smoothness of it. He said to himself, Good! and gave her nine points. And as James MacLiesh he saw, again and again and again, how beautiful she was. He said to himself, I am in love.

". . . butter wouldn't melt," said Harriet. "Never believe she's gone through two husbands already."

"*Norah?*" In his shock James tore his gaze from the ring for a second. Harriet gave a pleased little nod.

"Oh, yes," she said, "and that's not all. . . ."

But James was already back with Norah and the Swedish horse, as the elastic shoulder-in completed itself in a ten-meter circle, and then a flying, lengthened trot across the diagonal. He felt the places where Norah's concentration wavered. Each time the horse's drive escaped in some inaccuracy. He turned roughly, overshot a letter by a couple of strides, and began to work too fast. The lengthening of stride at the canter more nearly resembled a cavalry charge. James was close as the horse flew by down the rail. He heard the great rhythmic puffs of breath and saw the firm half halts, all too vigorous, all too necessary. Yet she did collect him to make the corner, and though he betrayed great excitement, she was able to guide him through the rest of the test without mishap.

The smile she put on, leaving the ring, was forced, and dropped off as soon as she passed through the gate. Yet she leaned forward, too, and clapped her gloved hand twice on the long, low neck of the tired horse.

Good! thought James. The horse deserved praise. His faults were generous, the result of too much energy rather than too little. A horse that gave too much could always be improved.

He turned away from the next competitor; a stingy horse,

executing the figures precisely in a dull pony gait; a bunchy rider with tight shoulders and no neck. He followed Norah at a discreet distance, delighting in the weary grace with which she swept the hat from her head.

". . . every single one! That's what I've heard."

How annoying! Harriet was still at his side. He looked at her, for the first time seeing that she wore riding clothes.

"When do you ride?" he asked, hoping it would be soon.

Harriet gave him a puzzled, annoyed look. "I ride in forty minutes," she said with utmost precision. "I asked you to do a little coaching, and you said yes."

So they weren't following Norah Craig. They were going to the barn.

Norah was going that way, too, with the black coat folded over one bare arm—hat, whip and reins all gracefully gathered in her hands; beside her, the man. They paced slowly, hips rolling, strides perfectly matched. Behind walked the Swedish horse, long and loose.

Snatches of talk drifted back, and James accelerated to eavesdrop.

". . . freight train," said Norah. Her voice was low and creamy. "I half-halted the hell out of him—"

"Yes, darling, that was painfully obvious. But what I'd like to point out is the extent to which he responded. Not enough, plainly, but he heard you this time. I see improvement."

"I let him get away from me," said Norah, her voice going deeper, as if it were difficult to admit a fault. "When my concentration was right, I had him."

James felt a little rise of heart, because he had sensed that. He understood her. . . .

So did the detestable man at her side. He slid an arm

around her waist and gave her a long, complicated look, full of sympathy for the trials in her life that might disturb her concentration, and of merry willingness to disturb her in a different way. For now he only kissed her cheek. "Have Jay cool him out and get Maia ready. I have to coach Evelyn now." He gave her a squeeze, and departed.

Walking captive beside Harriet, James half listened to her gossip till Norah disappeared around the corner of a barn. Then, spirits deflating, he began to hear again.

". . . did very well in the first divorce," said Harriet. "The second husband has money, too, but maybe he won't part with it so easily, because I hear they're patching things up."

"Was that guy the husband?"

Again he got the odd look. "*No*," said Harriet crisply. "Garry Kunstler, the trainer at Silver Thimble."

"Oh, yes, of course. Sorry."

So that was the famous Garry; hot local favorite among trainers and riding teachers, a name dropped reverently from every lip. Two years ago he'd been National Champion, Prix St. George, on his great horse Avatar.

No wonder . . .

"Anyway," said Harriet, "here's Devan. Help me saddle, will you, James?"

Devan was a MacLiesh Farm graduate; a small chestnut mare whose one fault had been her adamant refusal to enter a trailer. Tom MacLiesh had ridden her twenty-five miles home from the place where he bought her, and labored over her for months.

Like every horse that passed through MacLiesh hands, she had a certain potential—a decent build, decent gaits, the willing, teachable personality that Tom MacLiesh had a knack for spotting in the most unpromising places.

But ahead of them, as they made for an unoccupied slice of meadow in which to work, walked Garry Kunstler, beside a Hanoverian ten times the horse Devan was; stride like a young giraffe; mild, intelligent head; bloodlines back to the time of Fredrick the Great and beyond. . . . Devan seemed like a mustang off the range, and compared to that straight-backed redhead, poor old Harriet . . .

Well, Harriet was a tryer and Devan was an innocent, and they deserved his best, such as it was. "Here," he said, stopping, and shortening his field of vision to exclude Garry Kunstler.

"Trot around me a few—no, out farther. Okay."

Worse than he'd imagined. Harriet bounced and thumped and tugged, wearing a most professional and serious expression. She was obviously working very hard, and felt she knew what she was doing. Under this treatment, Devan moved with stilted, choppy strides, with high head and a distracted expression.

"*No!*" James cried. "Loosen up—no, be soft! Don't jab her mouth . . . keep *contact* with her! *No!*"

No good. He could not teach Harriet piecemeal, by correcting her every move. First she needed something inside; a model of correctness, a hero to imitate.

"Pretend you're Norah Craig!" he said. "Get a picture of Norah in your head!"

The corner of Harriet's mouth thinned derisively.

"Let *me* get on," cried James in desperation. There were fifteen minutes left before the test, and it was no time for a lesson; really, no chance of doing good. Yet he sensed in the current, attenuated Devan a perfect motion striving to be free.

He coaxed Harriet to the ground and mounted, crossing

the stirrups in front of the saddle. No time to waste adjusting them. He urged Devan forward.

She felt small and unsteady to him, liable to duck out from under him at any moment. She felt dull, rough, and jerky.

But . . . she was reins in his hands and a saddle beneath him, the hot smell of horse in his nostrils, the unseen body that seemed so naturally a part of his own. He felt alive again.

"Trot, Devan! Come on!"

Her response was meager, but he pushed, with legs, whip, seat, voice, and spirit. *"Trot, girl! Trot!"*

At last she began to fly, like a high-powered engine finding the range it was built for. Her ears flicked forward and back, expressing pleasure and disbelief. You mean you're *allowed* to go like this? Her stride became oily and powerful.

Now she wanted to get out of hand, but James balanced her with light checks and releases and small suppling circles. She didn't yet understand how to come against the bit and flex herself, like a drawn bow. She wanted to go through. James got her walking again, calmed her down, made her listen. At the corner of his eye he saw Harriet look at her watch.

"James, I've got to *go!*"

"Okay." He jumped down without touching the stirrups. His chest felt full of air, and his sneakered feet light.

"Up you go! You'll do fine. Remember, support her from behind, keep pushing. The judge wants to see impulsion."

Harriet gave him a tight-lipped glance and was silent.

James followed her toward the ring where the First Level test was running. First Level—he himself was now accomplished at First Level, able at last to be both bold and attentive to detail. He'd been reasonably confident of winning today; at least, of doing well enough to move Ghazal up and enter Second Level as a novice.

Next time. Next time.

Soon, then, he would compete against Norah Craig. Would he become as good as she was? Or would she be moving on, too, forever beyond him? Did it matter? He was never able to decide how much he cared about competition. You measured yourself against other riders, but the true measure was your horse, and that measure could be taken in private.

He spotted Gloria across the ring, face half hidden behind her camera. He wondered what she now saw through the lens. The grounds crew had done a nice job on this show, and as it was the first day, the tubs of geraniums were still fresh and the grass not much trampled. The low rail, a mere three inches off the turf, sparkled with fresh paint. It was the barest sketch of a fence, a symbol of the willing cooperation of the horses. James liked the rail. He hoped Gloria's pictures would say something about it.

A horse and rider left the ring, and now it was Harriet's turn. James stood close to the yellow rope, watching as she trotted Devan around the outside, awaiting the bell—dreading the bell. How grim she looked, unlike herself. The brief euphoria died in James's heart. Helplessly, guiltily, he watched the dynamic of frustration build itself. Harriet, knocked off-balance by his coaching, by the change he'd made in Devan—afraid, tight, clutching. Devan, also off-balance, full of go, resentful because she *knew* she should not be poky and dull but should fly—pulling on the bit, Harriet clutching, Devan shaking her head, swishing her tail, shying at the judge's trailer. . . . James tried to catch Harriet's eye as she passed, but she didn't see him.

"Hello," said a soft voice at his side. James spared a quick glance. Oh fine! he thought. The crowning pleasure of this glorious moment.

"Garry Kunstler," said the man, smiling and holding out his hand.

"James MacLiesh." They shook hands briefly, already turning back toward the ring.

"I saw you on that mare a few minutes ago," said Garry. "Good work!"

The bell tinkled. Horse and rider jumped. "I'm not so sure," said James.

"Oh, they're shaken up, of course. They'll do poorly. But . . ." Garry shrugged. "That's the price of learning."

"I'm not sure Harriet wants to pay," James said. "And I never asked."

He watched her enter the ring, making a wobbly line down the center, halting a few feet past *X*. A quick, jerky salute; the dropped hand leapt back to the rein. Then, mindful of James' injunction to push forward, she goosed Devan into a hasty trot.

"Oh, no!" James groaned.

"Not so bad. You've made a difference in that horse."

"Oh, yeah!" James agreed glumly as Harriet accomplished the most nearly triangular circle he'd yet seen. Then she set off down the rail. Devan was high-headed, leaning on the bit. Harriet leaned right back.

They took the corner without bending at all. "Oh, *Harriet!*" James groaned. "You're *so* awful!" Then, remembering the stranger at his side, "I shouldn't say that. She's a great person. . . ."

Garry shrugged, as if that mattered very little. True enough, James supposed. In the present circumstances Harriet's feisty and humorous personality made no difference at all. Feistiness and humor had drained away. She was pale and wide-eyed, passing him. Her ungloved hands showed white at the knuckle.

My fault, thought James. Poor Harriet!

Yet Devan looked better. Though awkward and out of control, she revealed the natural forward energy that Harriet had hitherto dampened.

You can save this, James telegraphed urgently to Harriet. Calm down and *think*! Get down in the middle of her—

Too late. Harriet failed to turn the corner; Devan hopped the white rail gaily, ears pricked and neck arched. Lighting on the other side, she gave a saucy snort and looked around for fresh worlds to conquer.

The judge's bell rang sharply, signaling disqualification as James turned from the yellow rope and hurried toward the gate. Norah Craig was in his way. He waited impatiently for her to pass and rushed to catch Devan's headstall, looking up at Harriet's angry, humiliated face.

It was a terrible moment. James felt every hour of the thirty-year difference in their ages, and his guilt quailed before her anger. He felt, too, how central they were in the public eye, and he had no notion what he was going to say. Yet something must be said, to save himself, to save face for Harriet, and to save for Devan the awkward progress she had made. He met Harriet's pebbly stare for some long seconds; then he blurted, "Harriet, I know you're upset, but she's really made a breakthrough!"

The corner of Harriet's mouth jumped. She pulled it back into line for a second, and then laughed reluctantly. "Yes, James, she certainly has!"

"No! I mean—look, come down here where I can talk to you!"

Harriet looked down on him for one more half-angry moment, tapping the long dressage whip on her thigh. Then she nodded and came down. Under the anger and the laugh, James sensed how shaken she was. Horribly contrite, and knowing himself in some measure forgiven, he put his arm around her shoulders and gave her a squeeze. At that moment he caught the eye of Garry Kunstler, standing near the gate watching. James flushed and led Harriet away.

"Sorry, I blew it for you. Do you ride tomorrow?"

"No, just the two today." She laughed, looking down at her boots. "Never mind, James. I blew the first one, too, all by myself."

"Well, then . . ." James took a deep breath. "I want you two to come down to us for some lessons—and before you say anything, the first couple are on the house. Okay? I owe you."

Harriet looked up, about to protest. She met James' eyes, hesitated, and said, "Yes."

"Good! You felt how much she's got in her—"

Harriet glanced at Devan, walking quietly beside her but with a lingering brightness in her eye. "Entirely different horse. She scared me to death."

"That's the horse she *should* be! That's how much she ought to give. And you can handle it, Harriet, once you know what to expect."

"Can I?" Harriet's voice was uncharacteristically low. "I'm a middle-aged accountant with chunky thighs, James, and I've been trying for a long time. I don't know if I can be any better."

Neither did James. Certainly he hadn't thought so half an hour ago. But now he had to make her better, and he frowned at her sternly. "*You* are fishing for compliments," he said. "Can you come Wednesday at three?"

"How about four?"

"All right, four. Without fail!"

Harriet was recovering and smiled at him indulgently, reminding him how young he was and that he was only male. "All right, Mr. MacLiesh. Without fail!" She led Devan away toward the barns.

Drained, James stood watching her go. He liked the way her head was high again, and her shoulders square. Good old Harriet!

"Well done!" said a soft voice at his shoulder, and he turned in astonishment to find Garry Kunstler.

He felt his brows shoot up and his face freeze haughtily. "I disagree," he said, and feeling he'd proven himself in every way a bastard, he turned to walk away, pretending to look for someone.

But Garry Kunstler was still at his side, speaking as if he hadn't heard the snub. "It's a fine line, of course, between teaching and manipulation. Horse or human, I feel it every day."

James slowed his steps. He knew he was being manipulated even now, but he was intrigued.

"I square it with myself," said Garry, "by remembering that they want this. Every horse knows in his bones what balance is. Every horse knows how to dance. If they were to live their lives in freedom, they wouldn't need teaching. But that's not how it is. I show them how to regain their natural balance under a rider, and they *want* to be balanced, because it's right."

"Hmm," said James, wondering. "And how do you square

with yourself about people?" He thought specifically of
Norah.

Garry smiled. "People *pay*," he said. "They're capable of
figuring me out and manipulating *me*, in their turn. I don't
worry so much about people."

They were threading slowly among the spectators, people
with dogs on leashes and people with babies in backpacks,
people loaded down with other people's coats, hats, numbers,
and bottles of fly spray. They came up now to another
stretch of yellow rope, beside a ring where Training Level
tests were in progress.

"Tell me about your place," said Garry. "I've heard of the
MacLieshes, of course, but till now I've never met one."

James's suspicions were conquered. Of course it's done deliberately, he reminded himself, but he didn't really care.
Eyes on the ring, taking in half consciously the soothing
rhythm of horses' legs in motion, he told Garry Kunstler
about MacLiesh Farm; his work with Ghazal and Robbie,
and the various spoiled horses; his hopes, his ambitions.
Garry listened and asked illuminating questions.

The last thing he asked was, "Have you ever ridden an
upper-level horse?"

James was distracted for a second. Across the ring, he spotted Gloria, homing in on him with her zoom lens. "Uh—
no," he said, frowning back at her. "No, I haven't."

"Would you like to?"

He had gained every scrap of James's attention.

"I don't ride my top horse till tomorrow. He needs exercise."

"But *why*? I mean . . ." Just twang on this Stradivarius a
couple times! Tool my Rolls around the block!

"Someone did the same for me once. Let's just say I'm passing it along. Will you?"

"Well—*yes*! Hell, yes!"

Garry laughed. "Well, come on, then!"

The Silver Thimble horses were stabled in the farthest, quietest barn. They had taken over a full dozen stalls, including one for tack and one for a dressing room. Yet despite this ample storage space, supple, expensive saddles were hung on outside racks, and blue-and-silver coolers, blankets, and pads were draped richly everywhere, like the banners of a secluded kingdom. A stretch of several empty stalls separated Silver Thimble from the ragtag and bobtail in the rest of the barn.

It's only money, thought James, resisting. Yet his eye was seduced by Norah Craig, polishing a big, calm warm-blood with a blue-and-silver cloth. His ear was seduced by the serenity.

A little unfocused, he watched Garry speak to Norah and to the young man, Jay, then go to the tack stall and bring out a grooming kit and halter. He set the kit down at the hitch rail and approached a stall with a bronze nameplate that read AVATAR.

No, I'm reading that wrong! James narrowed his eyes and went a couple of steps nearer.

No, I'm *not* reading it wrong! He looked up as a noble, dark head appeared above the nameplate; a gleaming head with a knife blade of white down the frontal bone. The head was as familiar to him as those of his own horses. He'd seen it in sports magazines dozens of times over the past three years: Avatar, National Champion, Prix St. George.

The great horse nickered like any Shetland pony at the approach of his master, and graciously gave his head to be haltered. Garry opened the door. Released from paralysis, James stepped forward.

"Sir—uh—Garry . . . are you sure? I mean . . . what if I screw him up?"

Garry looked amused. "This is an intelligent and highly educated animal, Mr. MacLiesh. I don't think you'll find him easy to lead astray."

"But—"

"Norah rides him."

"Norah's Second Level! I'm nowhere *near* as good as she is!"

"At your age I don't see how you could be." Garry led the beautiful horse forth to the hitch rail. "So start with one of the soft brushes, will you? And hand me one."

"But—"

"As you know quite well—remember, I *have* seen you ride—dressage is the continuing refinement and elaboration of certain fundamentals; a steady seat, good legs, sensitive hands, and the pure natural gaits of the horse. Avatar remembers all about First Level work. So really, I don't quite see what you're fussing about."

Put that way, neither did James. In silence he brushed the silken, sensitive hide. He found the spot, just behind the whithers, that liked to be scratched, and he watched the great horse grimace and wiggle his lip.

A great horse is just like any other horse, he thought. Only more so. Yet even in this prosaic scratch response there was a statement. He thought of Ghazal, who projected dignity with every gesture. He did not yet know what Avatar was saying.

Horse Man

He stood back now as Garry girthed on a magnificent long-skirted saddle; the best saddle, soft as a glove. Then the bridling; the dark horse reached willingly for the bits and savored them on his tongue, clanking the snaffle. His head came up and his ears pricked. His eyes began to dream.

"Come on," said Garry. "We'll find a relatively private spot."

"All I have is sneakers," said James, lifting one. Somehow he hoped for a delay.

"Never mind, you won't be using stirrups."

Oh.

Delay came from Norah, asking a question as they were walking away. Garry gave the reins to James and stepped apart with her.

James stood waiting, in an absolute daze. His eye was torn between the great horse and the beautiful woman, so that he really saw neither. Only as the conversation between Garry and Norah ended, and the reins were taken from him, did he see Gloria, alone at the hitch rail, lowering the camera from her face. She smiled and waved at him.

Now what was she up to? Lately she did what she called photographic essays. James thought of this day, all the fatuous, forlorn, and foolish ways his own image would appear in the developing pan, and blushed.

But they were walking; past the three rings where tests were being held, past horses warming up and cooling out, past picnickers and gossipers ahorse and afoot. Far out at the end of the fields a fat, lopsided old woman leaned on two canes and shouted directions to three riders circling her, two men and a girl. Before they reached this group, Garry veered left, and they crossed the shallow brook, coming out into a small meadow screened from view by trees. Garry stopped to tighten the girth and pull the stirrups down. James looked back and saw Gloria on the path behind him.

"Mr. MacLiesh." Garry stood at the horse's head like a groom. His strange gnomelike face was quite inscrutable. James felt his heart thump in his chest.

He gathered the reins and set his foot to the stirrup, hesitated a second and swung up. He lit on the marvelous saddle with an instant sense of homecoming.

"Cross the stirrups in front," Garry directed. James obeyed. Then he combed his fingers through the double set of reins, organizing them and finding the horse's mouth.

Garry stepped back. "Just warm him up a few minutes." The meadow sloped steeply. The man considered a moment. "Down here, on the level."

Now. James squeezed gently with his legs, feeling as gauche as a boy on his first pony. Yet, pony or Prix St. George, the principle was the same. The great horse stepped out.

It was a bold, lithe walk, the horse as loose at the shoulder as a tiger. James felt high off the ground and tippy. He tried unobtrusively to adjust his seat, and as he did, he felt the horse slide to the left in a smooth leg yield.

Now why in hell had he done that? He froze his seat bones to immobility. The horse stopped and squared up.

James felt the heat rise to his face. He squeezed his legs, intending to walk again.

Instead, he achieved a canter from the standstill. In the great bounding transition, even as he threw his hands forward to avoid jabbing the horse's mouth, he felt that his left leg was fractionally behind his right. Avatar had felt this and assumed it to be intentional.

All right, he knew when he was licked. He slowed and

then stilled his seat, bringing the horse to a halt. Then, moving only his head, he turned to look back at Garry.

The man's face was lit with amusement. "Well? You know what the problem is, don't you?"

"Yes, but—"

"So sit still! Try some circles at a trot."

James took a deep breath and rearranged his jutting jaw. He felt trapped and foolish.

Deliberately he took himself back a couple of notches. What was the true situation? He was not here to impress Garry Kunstler. He sat astride the great horse Avatar, by unlooked-for chance. The opportunity must not be wasted.

All right, relax.

His belly softened. The fork of his seat sank down into the saddle. All at once he felt the heat of the horse's body against his calves.

Laying his palm on the glossy neck that rose before him, he said, "Hello. I'm James MacLiesh."

He sensed a change, perhaps a softening. Now he offered the suggestion, "Trot?"

They trotted.

Oh, wow! thought James. Oh, *wow!* The saddle hugged him close and deep, and he was part of this springy forward trot. Part of it, so that his suggestion that they turn and describe a circle on the hoof-marked grass was perhaps no suggestion at all but a shared idea arising in the combined mind/body of horse and man. Horse and man. Horse-man.

Several round, beautiful circles; then changing direction, crossing the circle in a fat *S*, dividing the circle yin and yang; then around again. A rush of air to the chest—a clear, pure stillness. A silent shout for joy.

Adding to the combined consciousness came a voice, instructing James to do things he'd never done before, saying how. As the words came, James acted, with no delay for thinking; collected trot, piaff, passage, and pirouette. Lovely, lovely pirouette, the horse cantering gaily in place around his own back legs, all the energy he was capable of compressed between the rider's legs and his hands. . . .

Horses are heavier than words. A horse cannot canter the pirouette as lightly as you can say it. His lightness is the lightness of half a ton. His breath gusts out with the great effort, and the fun of lifting himself, of falling to earth, of lifting again. James had always wanted to ride a pirouette. Because he never had, did not know how, he had imagined it to be impossible. Never mind that he had seen it many times. He knew horses to be too heavy. Now he knew how very nearly that was true. Marvelous . . .

Then release, like an arrow shot from the bow, across the little meadow to the end. Hurrah! Turn and walk slowly back along the brook with the reins all long and floppy. Black ears go east and west like a plow horse's, black neck low, black nose stretching forward in snorts of satisfaction.

His shirt clung, front and back. Dust prickled on his sweating brow. He began to have thoughts.

Such as, Boy! Oh, boy!

And more complex ideas; the realization of what had been done for him. He had been given a gift of understanding. Someday, when he brought Ghazal to this level, he would remember the feeling of today and measure against it.

He understood, too, that this marvelous ride had been far from the partnership of real dressage. Avatar had done all these things because he understood and loved them. He knew how to be beautiful and required from a rider only the patterns in which to enact his beauty.

Garry had made him so, and Garry could lift him higher, make him still more beautiful and correct. James MacLiesh, as yet, was only along for the ride.

So it was like a pony ride, or like sitting on your father's lap with your hands on the wheel as he guides the car gently down the driveway. Not an accomplishment but a look ahead at what you will do one day when you are grown.

He came to Garry and dismounted. The three of them, all separate again, stood looking at one another. Was there anything to say?

Apparently not. Garry gave his hand and James shook it. The man took the reins of his horse, mounted, and rode away.

James stood alone when they had gone, his back to the path. The feeling of that ride slowly drained out of his body, and he felt a yearning, painful joy, like unrequited love.

It reminded him of the morning's pain, in that empty gap between competitors. Could he say, now, that it was all for the best? He had seen Norah and ridden Avatar. He had upset Harriet and helped Devan, been humbled by a cousin and a camera, and then been lifted up by Mr. Garry Kunstler of Silver Thimble Farm. Would he trade all this for three five-minute rides before a judge and before his peers, a few numbers written up publicly on a board beside his name?

Yes, he thought he would. He was glad the choice had not been given.

He turned to go. Gloria was coming toward him on the path, and the fat old woman was going the opposite way. Garry Kunstler, now dismounted, walked slowly at her side, his head inclined in courteous listening.

Nearing Gloria, James saw as freshly as the first time her round bright face, so full of strength and cheer. The camera

47

lifted briefly; she took another picture of him. Then she snapped the case shut and switched the strap to her shoulder. With the camera she put away the something in her manner that said she was at work.

"Tell me," she said, "all about it!"

"Later," said James. "When you show me your pictures."

EXTENDED FAMILY

THE SUMMER FOLLOWING Puttins' death was long and angry.

My father was always home—the worst thing about a parent who is also a teacher. He golfed. He kept a keen eye on the depth of the lawn and ordered someone to mow whenever it exceeded half an inch. He organized us to help Mum clean the spotless house. He read ugly, depressing books by B. F. Skinner and tried to push them onto me.

That summer I couldn't bear to disagree in silence. That summer I knew I was *right*, at least more right than he was, and I couldn't stand not to tell him so.

That got Greg mad. He cares about keeping the surface

smooth, so he can glide beneath and tend his own affairs. But when one of us quarrels with Dad, he gets super-alert to disobedience and disrespect. Greg found himself curtailed.

"Why can't you just keep your mouth shut?" he kept muttering to me that summer. "Kris, keep your fat mouth shut!"

He sat beside me at meals and kicked me, until I sang out loud and clear, "Greg, why are you kicking me?" Once was always enough.

Aunt Mil was often the subject of the quarrel. I spent too much time with her, she was the source of my cockeyed ideas, she was a sentimental and senile old woman who doted on cats to an unhealthy degree . . . on and on.

One afternoon I was discussing with Mum—or rather, *to* Mum, who heard one word in ten—Aunt Mil's refusal to think about getting a kitten. "She keeps saying she's too old," I said, "and she doesn't want to get started loving something new. But I think it would do her good to have a kitten. She's dwelling so much on the past right now, she should have a little thing that doesn't have a past, only a future—"

"What kind of a future?" asked my father, coming out of *Beyond Freedom and Dignity* in his alert way. "The first thing you'll do is take the poor creature to be surgically sterilized, thereby depriving it of its main function in life. What kind of a future is that?"

"They don't care about that," I said. "They don't miss what they've never had."

"Ah, Kris! Would you allow that argument if we were discussing, say, slavery?"

"That's different!"

"Of course it's different, but the argument is just as specious."

He was right about that, maybe, but his analogy didn't fit the case. He's expert at that sort of arguing; unbeatable if allowed to frame the issue in his own terms.

He went on. "It's a bit sickening, I find, the way you pet lovers take despotic control of an animal's life in the name of kindness. Why shouldn't a cat live a raucous, fertile life and die young? It's the natural way."

"Why shouldn't you and Mum have thirteen kids instead of only three? That's natural too!" My voice was high and shaky with anger. Dad smiled calmly.

"The difference is that we made the choice ourselves."

"Animals can't make that choice, but why should their health be put in jeopardy because of that? Why should they be allowed to overpopulate?" I saw him flinch and knew I'd found my fighting point. "You always talk about those Third World countries and how they should be made to control their birthrate. Isn't it the same thing?"

It wasn't the same; I saw that even as I spoke. People can understand the concept of birth control, and do something about it. Animals apparently cannot. I was arguing as he does, from a false analogy. It worked as well for me as it did for him.

He glared at me speechlessly for a few moments. "Young lady," he said finally, "I suggest you go out and trim the hedge, as I told you yesterday, instead of lazing around in here being disrespectful."

One for me!

When I came in an hour later for a glass of lemonade, he looked up from his book and said, "It's called pedomorphy, Kris. All domestic animals are selectively bred never to grow up, so humans can dominate them. Now I know what I'd call that if it were done to people."

"They grow up!"

"Oh, yes, but they stay cute, don't they, the dear doggies and kitties! They keep their round skulls and their big eyes, and they love to play. It's a mother's dream, isn't it? 'Oh, if only they'd *stay* at this stage,'" he quoted squeakily. Mum, knitting on the couch and watching her soap opera, flushed.

"I don't see why *you* should care," I said. "That book you're reading says freedom and dignity don't exist even for humans, so why should you care about animals?"

"I don't care," said my father smugly. "It's a matter of aesthetics. If we must have sappiness and baby talk in this world, I prefer it confined to real babies and not made-up ones."

One for him.

I couldn't deny the truth of it. Put the average dog beside the average wolf and the difference is clear. The dog is a foolish adolescent, the wolf a clearheaded, independent adult.

With cats it isn't so simple. They're capable of switching on and off, like people. But they aren't the same as they would be naturally, on their own.

"So what?" said Aunt Mil when I told her about this argument. "You're not the same as if you'd never met me, are you? And you're not the same as if you lived in Ohio, or went to boarding school. It doesn't mean a thing."

"No?" I didn't find that totally comforting. I like to think it means something, that I am who I am.

Still, since we live in town, for instance, I'm not horse-crazy, though I go riding whenever I can. I even cultivate friendships with people I might otherwise ignore, if they happen to have horses. This is one way circumstance has formed me.

Extended Family

This afternoon, we were driving to the farm of one of these people, Karen Blake, who isn't very interesting but does have a couple of Morgans. Unbeknownst to Aunt Mil, she also had a litter of kittens the right age for adopting. As I had it planned, Aunt Mil was to hang around in the company of the kittens while Karen and I rode. By the time we got back, it would be all over. At least one kitten would come home with us.

Karen had the horses tied out front when we arrived. Aunt Mil went to their heads and talked to them. "My father had a team of Morgans," she told Karen. I remembered them from the photo album: a cheeky-looking pair, with ears always going two ways at once. The girl in the shapeless white dress and tousled hair, always somewhere near, was little Millie— Aunt Mil to be.

It was pleasant to see how she treated the horses—rather brusque, rather bossy. "Yes, I know you're silly," she told Star, who was sniffing her face and rolling big brown eyes. "Of course you're a pig," she said to Beauty, who poked hopefully at her pocket. Star and Beauty—those names tell you a lot about Karen Blake.

Karen was fussing around in the shed getting brushes. The horses kept an eye on her, and when she passed the grain barrel, Star flung up her head and nickered loudly.

"It's all right," Karen called. "Mother's coming!"

It was the sort of thing I was used to from Karen. Alone, I never would have given it a thought. But I chanced to be looking at Aunt Mil, and I saw an expression of almost physical disgust cross her face. For a second she looked nauseous.

Karen bustled up, chattering. "Poor Star, did you want your Mummy? There, baby, Mummy's here—"

"Kris," said Aunt Mil in a faint, throttled voice, "I think

I'll go do some shopping. Pick you up in an hour." And before I could utter more than a half syllable of protest, she was gone.

I turned back to Karen, still babbling of mummies and babies to the horses, each of whom weighed ten times what she did; fat, frisky, bursting with greed, and entirely self-centered. Even as I looked, a beautiful fluffy kitten toddled out from under the shed stairs. They'll be here when she gets back, I thought. But I no longer felt hopeful, and for once the horseback ride seemed more chore than pleasure.

We returned from our ride to find Aunt Mil waiting in the car. She waved and called, "Take your time, Kris!" Then she went back to her newspaper. Unobserved, the kittens rolled and skirmished in the shed. With their wild ears and wicked, glaring eyes, they looked murderous; crouching, wiggling briefly, and then launching themselves on one another, biting down through the billowing fluff of stomachs, necks, and haunches with their tiny, needle-like teeth. It was an orgy of slaughter, and all wasted. Aunt Mil wouldn't even look.

As I started to lead Beauty to the pasture the mother cat came padding up the driveway, slow and heavy-bodied, bringing a mouse. She called to the kittens with her mouth full, and they didn't hear her till she was quite close. Then they all trotted toward her, their thin tails bent so far over their backs that the tips almost touched their ears. It was a funny caricature of the way a confident cat greets you, tail as straight as a flagpole, like a giggle or a big goofy grin instead of a hello. It seemed to express the utmost confidence, as you would expect between mother cat and kittens.

She dropped her mouse, and the kittens sniffed it dubiously, looking at her. Awfully big and hairy, wasn't it? What are you supposed to do with this?

Mama made no attempt to teach them. She stretched out on the driveway and yawned a wide pink yawn. Tough work!

Aunt Mil drove me back to her place, where I was to mow the lawn and start scraping the back of the house. This work, and the generous wage she pays, are the reasons I'm allowed to spend so much time with Aunt Mil.

Robert stood up to greet us as we got out of the car, stretching his back legs out behind as if they were caught in molasses. His fat tiger-tail nearly touched his shoulder blades, and he looked straight into our faces, his eyes yellow suns of love and trust.

"*He* thinks you're his mother," I said.

Aunt Mil's hand froze under Robert's white chin. Still bent over, she looked up at me.

"He and I both know the difference," she said.

Her eyes held mine. I saw they were a little bloodshot in the corners; old eyes. Angry eyes. She was facing me down the way Dad does sometimes. With Dad the issue is dominance. I never look away, and now, startled, I held Aunt Mil's gaze until her attention was claimed by Robert. She completed the chin scratch to his satisfaction and straightened up, moving away from me as she said, "This girl Karen doesn't seem to be a good influence."

From a parent that would have sent me through the ceiling. From a *parent* it wouldn't be unexpected. But Aunt Mil has been in the habit of treating me as a rational being.

Following her into the house, I said, "I didn't mean *you* thought it."

I received no reply, not even a look, and I said no more. My voice had sounded so conciliatory. I felt like a scolded child who seeks an approving word, no matter how irrelevant. So I shut up, went out, and mowed the lawn, then scraped paint for an hour. Inside, I heard Aunt Mil vacuuming and washing dishes. All the time I scraped, I waited for her to come out. She didn't. Robert came instead, to climb the ladder and sit on the little paint shelf, blinking chummily.

After an hour I put the ladder away and went inside. Gingersnaps were in the oven, but Aunt Mil looked stern and remote. Again I wanted to ingratiate myself. Instead, I told her, "I have to go watch the house. No one's home tonight."

"I thought that didn't matter," said Aunt Mil, but not quickly or warmly enough.

"I need to go to the library too," I said. When she didn't press further, I left.

Other people run to the candy store or shopping mall when hurt and uncertain. I run to the library. Today was Saturday, which meant short hours, and I arrived with only fifteen minutes to spare. I went to my favorite section, and the books I chose were old friends. They were certainties, and they were chosen by weight and shape, the maximum number that fit in the bike basket.

Home, to let myself in with the hidden key—placed where every thief ought to look first, under the rubber mat. Home by myself, to the forbidden luxuries of ice-cream sodas for supper, of lying with my feet on the sacred sofa, and of reading six animal books straight through without paternal comment.

As with most forbidden luxuries, they proved cloying. Ice-cream sodas leave a sensation of tooth decay, the couch becomes uncomfortable, and six animal books mean six sets of assumptions, six different ways of being made to feel uneasy.

I got up and brushed my teeth, thinking of telepathic German shepherds and the blind instinct of beavers building dams, the issue of animal consciousness, the way pets manipulate owners by playing sick . . .

Oh, dear! Maybe I should become a plain old veterinarian; deal with animals' bodies and forget about their minds, if any.

I could think of no more forbidden pleasures I felt like engaging in. Under other circumstances I might have biked over to Aunt Mil's. I wouldn't have minded a gingersnap and some rational conversation. Now I turned on the television and checked out all the boring channels, turned it off again, and roamed through the empty house, sad and full of wishes.

On the kitchen table lay the spare key. Better conceal it again, so the burglars can find it and not have to smash a window. I snapped on the yard light and stepped outside.

A sound came from near the hedge, and then a listening silence.

I went cold, as if dashed with a bucket of ice water. Nine o'clock in the suburbs, house lights all around—I should jump inside and lock the door; call a neighbor, call the police. Yet I stood rooted with all my senses wide, like a traveler beside a lonely campfire, waiting.

The sound repeated, and my eyes flew to the spot, halfway down the hedge from where I stood. Small white feet, enormous white whiskers—oh! Cat!

I relaxed so quickly that I sat down *plunk* on the cement steps. The feet vanished out of the circle of light.

"Oh, don't be afraid! Here, kitty!"

57

THE SIXTH SENSE

I heard the nice-nice, high-pitched sound of my own voice, as if with my father's ears. Gag!

We pitch the voice instinctively higher when speaking to babies, and with good reason, science now tells us. The little things actually respond better to baby talk. But why do it with cats? Was there a parallel?

I could see again the two white semicircles of toes.

"Hi, cat," I said, trying to speak normally. "What's up? You live around here?" Flat, regular people voice. It sounded dumb, and the cat moved no closer.

"This isn't an animal house," I said, going up the scale a little. "Nothing to feed you. No food for kitties!"

I must have glanced away for a second, though I didn't think so. The cat now sat full in the light, as if she had moved forward without getting to her feet.

She was a trim little half-grown kitten, black with white bib and whiskers. Her white paws were placed primly side by side. Her slanting eyes never left me for an instant, even when her face split wide in a sharp-toothed yawn.

Kitten for Aunt Mil! In a split second I played through the laborious taming, the presentation, the apology and reconciliation, and the growth of the kitten into a cat of fragrant individuality.

"Here, kitty," I called, and stretched my hand out coaxingly. The kitten vanished out of the light.

Well, just sit and call. She'll come again. She had moved in synchrony with my advances and retreats, as if bound by a magnetic field. So I sat back on the steps and called sweetly, full of confidence.

The wait stretched long. The circle of light remained empty.

After a time I began to feel deflated, and the cement steps

grew hard. I pushed the key under the mat, getting ready to stand up and still looking out at the lawn. Then something made me glance into the shadowed breezeway. Not twelve feet away sat the little cat.

She seemed unlikely to be startled now; settled down, paws folded, watching. How long had she been there? I imagined how quickly she must have nipped around the back of the house, running low to the ground in the drip line under the eaves, outwitting me.

We studied each other like a pair of philosophers, each awaiting the other's pronouncement on Life. The kitten spoke first, lips drawing back just enough to emit a threadlike cry. It didn't seem to be a plea for anything, just a comment.

"Ridiculous," I told her. "Cats are just gene machines. They don't have anything to say."

She cried again, narrowing her eyes at me in a smug expression.

"You can't make choices, you know. You run totally by instinct."

The kitten's third comment was identical to the first two.

"Okay, suppose I said you're a higher being and you can communicate telepathically? Hmm?

"I'm waiting."

Before the kitten's message could burst full-blown upon my brain, I heard a call out across the backyards. "Thea! Thea!" The kitten's black ear twitched.

"That's you, isn't it? I thought you were a waif."

"*Thea!*" called the voice—a hushed, young male voice trying to shout softly, to reach the desired ears and no others. Flick! went the kitten's ear in slight annoyance.

"Aren't you going to go?"

The caller had now turned up our street. I could hear the stifled irritation in his voice, and also the anxiety. The kitten glanced out the opening of the hedge for a second, then turned away. She aimed her tiny face at me and began to purr, like an air conditioner coming on.

"Pretty hard-hearted, aren't you?" But I was hard-hearted myself, and instead of rising and calling out, I waited on the steps. "Thea, *dammit!*" said the voice, and then a blond head, shining in the streetlight, peered cautiously around the end of the hedge.

"Brrt!" cried the kitten in a tone of glad surprise. She jumped to her feet and ran to him.

I stood, too, happy to get up off the hard cement. "She heard you all the time," I said.

The boy looked up in surprise. The kitten was rubbing around him ecstatically, rising on her hind legs to push her head into his hand and purring loudly.

"Don't be taken in," I said. "She sat here on the breezeway the whole time you were calling."

The boy picked her up and put her on his shoulder. Still purring, she wrapped her paws around his head as far as she could reach and tried to gnaw his ear off. He asked through a grimace, "How'd you find her?"

"She was out here when I opened the door. She didn't ask to come in or anything. We just sat and visited a while."

He smiled at that, and I realized how foolish I must sound, babbling away to a perfect stranger. I tried to find a way to stop.

"Yeah, but . . . like I said, she heard you all the time. She was just waiting till you got here." Oh, God, Kris, *shut up!*

"Yeah," said the boy, "they have their own agendas." He detached the kitten from his ear and cradled her upside down on one arm, tickling her stomach while she chewed and kicked his hand. "Anyway, thanks for keeping her busy till I caught up. We just moved in yesterday—I don't think she knows where to come back to yet."

"Oh, she's a pretty wise little customer."

"Yeah, she is," said the boy, smiling at me while his hands battled the kitten. "Anyway, thanks!" He moved away down the street, and I went slowly inside.

He'll be going to our school in the fall, I bet.

I fell asleep thinking over the conversation and awoke in the morning on the phrase, *They have their own agendas.*

The sun was shining, and snores down the hall told me that Mum and Dad had come in late, without disturbing me in the slightest. It was too nice a morning to hold a grudge. I ate a yogurt out on the steps and then biked over to Aunt Mil's.

Aunt Mil, I decided, had spoken without thinking yesterday and had continued not to think. Of course, she wouldn't apologize, and I didn't care. If it happened again, I'd bring her up pretty sharply, that's all.

Aunt Mil, I decided, was being as willfully blind as my father. But I could change her mind, more likely, because with her I could insist on being treated as a person instead of a project. Besides, I had a trick or two up my sleeve.

Other things I decided on the twenty-minute bike ride were that the kitten Thea was likely to return, that next time I would find out the boy's name, and that I liked the way I looked—straight and strong and sort of handsome-plain—and maybe he would too. I decided I was now old enough to admit to thinking about boys.

Early as it was, I found Aunt Mil in the garden. She's somewhat obsessive about work; a person in her early eighties has something to prove every single day. She has her pride, too, as people exclaim over her gardens and point her out to their friends. Then, too, she doesn't need as much sleep anymore. She thinks she's supposed to accomplish some spiritual growth during this period, and worries if she's doing it.

She straightened at my call with only the barest suggestion of stiffness, and her smile was everything I'd hoped for.

"You're early, Kris. Have you had breakfast?"

"Sort of."

"Me too. Let's sort of have it again."

Over the good homemade toast and strawberry jam, and fresh dark cherries from the backyard tree, I told her about Thea and the boy. I enjoyed going over it again, with Aunt Mil smiling at all the right parts.

Just as we were finishing, the phone rang. I jumped and wasn't surprised that the caller was my father. Aunt Mil made soothing sensible noises and turned him over to me.

"It was very irresponsible of you not to leave a note," was his greeting.

"I forgot. But you knew where I was."

"I surmised you'd be there, since that's where you spend seventy percent of your time. I'd be a lot happier, Kris, if you had friends your own age."

"I have friends my own age! You don't like them!"

"Oh, that foolish Karen—"

"Karen's all right!" I said.

"Yes, Karen's all right, and so is your Aunt Mil, but not quite so much of her. I must say, I would have thought a woman her age would encourage you to be more responsible.

Extended Family

We'll be seeing you sometime this week, I presume?" Without waiting for an answer, he hung up.

Aunt Mil was at the sink washing dishes. I went to dry, trying to clamp down on everything inside me, not to let her know the things he had said. We worked quietly for a couple of minutes. Then, as Aunt Mil turned off the faucet, she said, "I suspect he's rather jealous, Kris."

"I hate him!"

She didn't jump in to correct me. In the silent space she left, I was able to wonder in what degree it was true. How much did I hate my father? Did I love him at all? I remember loving him as a little girl. I've seen pictures of me on his lap, him smiling at me.

Aunt Mil sighed, staring into space as she slowly dried her hands. "I sometimes wonder how that man manages to teach."

"Some people say he's all right."

"Yet he does so badly with you. He cares, he wants you to come out right, but he's so clumsy."

"He hates me to come here."

"Well," said Aunt Mil, sounding unusually tolerant, "I don't think he quite sees me as a member of the family. If I lived with you, it might be different."

"Huh?"

"In earlier times, Kris, an old widow like me wouldn't live alone. Since I have no children of my own, I'd probably live with my nearest relative: your mother. In a situation like that, your father probably wouldn't notice if you and I preferred each other's company."

"The extended family," I said, to show I knew what she was talking about.

She took me up on that, with a sharp, alert look that momentarily reminded me of my father. "That's what they call it nowadays, but that's sloppy thinking. I suspect the modern arrangements fit that description more accurately. Families are extended over great distances of space and culture, and I think they're stretched too thin. The old way seems more nuclear, in the sense of being clustered around a center."

"I never thought of it that way."

"I know you didn't. Watch out for words, Kris. They're not things; they're ways of referring *to* things. You must always ask yourself if they are accurate."

"But you have to use the same words other people do," I said experimentally. "You have to be understood."

"Compromise exists," Aunt Mil allowed after considering a moment. "As long as you're clear in your own mind, and you're sure you're getting through. But I find it's usually best to be explicit if at all possible. It saves time later on."

She had taken the sting out of the morning. As we separated, each to her own work, I wondered what it would be like if Aunt Mil lived with us.

Fights. Even under the same roof, she and my father would never agree. But there were fights now, so that was no different. Rational conversation at any hour of the day. Without a doubt there would be a cat. There would be more, and better, books. Home would be rich, complex, and interesting.

Family, to me, is a threatening word. It means being boxed in with a few people you didn't choose, who don't understand you, who have authority over you, who bore and stifle you, who are in every way insufficient.

But what if those few people didn't have to be sufficient? What if they included the parents of your best friends, and the best friends of your parents, all those honorary aunts and uncles; Aunt Dot, say, who was the person to call if you were sick at school and nobody was home to come for you? Or Uncle Pete, that wisecracking college friend of Dad's. Or . . .

Something bumped my ladder and slipped silkenly past my legs—Robert, hopping onto the paint shelf with tail erect, eyes hot and golden and full of self. What was Robert saying, greeting me as a kitten greets its mother? Was he naming me "Aunt Kris"?

How Aunt Mil would shudder! But I looked down into Robert's beaming eyes and thought, They have their own agendas.

So did I.

Ten-thirty came—a good time, and half this side of the house was scraped. "Aunt Mil," I called. "D'you think you could drive me over to Karen's?"

Aunt Mil was in harmony with me this morning, and unsuspicious. She didn't ask why I was going on Sunday, which I usually don't. She didn't remember that Karen's family goes to church every Sunday, and then has dinner with her grandparents. She just sank her trowel up to the hilt in the good loose dirt and came along.

Karen's house is at the top of a steep, tree-lined driveway, in its own little world. All the long swoop upward I held my breath, but their car was not in the yard. So far so good.

When the old VW stopped wheezing, the yard was beautifully still, with an old-fashioned Sunday peace. Wind ruffled the treetops and stirred the chimes. The two horses grazed on the skyline, and deep in the shed I saw the white flash of a kitten at play.

I got slowly out of the car. My heart was pounding. I'm not used to deceiving people, particularly Aunt Mil.

"Hmm," I said. "I wonder where everyone is." I went to the door and knocked, crossing my fingers that nobody had stayed behind. But the knock flattened to nothing in the empty house, and I went back to the car.

"They must have gone out for a minute. Do you mind if we wait?"

"Not for a little while," said Aunt Mil. She reached for a magazine from the littered backseat.

Damn! I didn't think of that.

I wandered into the shed, trying to think what to do. The kittens bounced out and swirled in wild play around my ankles. They made me feel like a giantess. Amazing, that these tiny animals should have such confidence in the huge members of another species! What does it mean, to be of another species? Which is greater, the sum of the differences or the sum of what we hold in common?

As if they'd sensed something interesting going on, older cats began to converge; mother and a couple of uncles, gathering casually from different points. One kitten reared on its hind legs to grab the neck of a huge, fluffy uncle, biting fiercely for the jugular. Uncle flattened kitten for an aggressive bath, frequently punctuated with bites.

"Aunt Mil," I called. "Come see the cats."

I think perhaps she'd been watching already, over the top of the magazine. The magazine was old, and the day too fine for reading. But as she got slowly out of the car, I began to see suspicion on her face.

"Are you sure Karen's expecting you?" she asked.

"I *thought* so," I said, sounding innocent and troubled.

"Well—" said Aunt Mil, and had to stop, as a kitten pounced on her moving foot. For a second she arched up a little, ready to spit. But she thought again, stooped, and stroked it with one finger. The kitten rose in pleasure under her hand, starting to purr.

Instantly the other kittens converged, curious. They tumbled and stroked themselves around Aunt Mil's hand, some gazing up at her face, others seeming to regard the hand as the total creature, the feet and face as other things entirely.

The mother cat pulled herself up from her sprawl on the cool, packed earth of the shed floor. She was a big brilliant calico, warm marmalade-orange and black, with dramatic splashes of white. She ambled toward Aunt Mil with an air of unworried responsibility, coming to check out her children's new playmate.

Two kittens saw and trotted to her, tails high in happy expectation. As they bumped their heads under her chin, I looked up to see Aunt Mil watching.

"There!" I said. "That's just the way Robert greeted you. See?"

Her eyes flew to mine, startled and growing cold. "I see indeed," she said, glancing around the yard. "I take it we do not expect Karen after all?"

"Aunt Mil—"

"Kris," she said, "I do not use my cats as substitute children."

I suddenly felt how possible it was to be furious with Aunt Mil. It was frightening—the kind of fury I'd felt so far only toward my father, the fury of a perfectly good argument denied a chance. I paused to steady myself, to find the exact thing I wanted to say. I held her eye all the while, trying for an expression of friendly challenge.

"I didn't say anything about what *you* think," I said finally. "I'm talking about what *they* think."

That interested her, but not quite enough.

"You can define the relationship any way you want," I said, "but if you don't give the animal what it needs, it'll look somewhere else. Like me."

"Like you?" asked Aunt Mil quickly.

"Well, I can't get any rational conversation at home, so I come to you. It's like what we were talking about this morning, the extended family. All I'm saying is, we aren't the only ones defining things. Cats have their own agendas, and *I* think they're including us in some extended family structure of their own."

No response.

"Like lions," I said. "Like a pride."

Aunt Mil's gaze dropped from me to the group of cats at our feet; a knot of tussling kittens, Uncle still engaged in a bath-fight, Mama and another uncle washing each other's faces affectionately. Quite a social whirl, for animals traditionally described as aloof and solitary. Watching them, Aunt Mil sank without seeming to realize it onto an upturned apple crate.

"It's not unscientific," I said as the silence stretched. "Konrad Lorenz talks about stuff like this all the time—how animals fit you into their social structure. . . ."

Aunt Mil glanced up at me, her naturally down-curved mouth breaking into a smile that just passed the sour point. "All right, Kris, all right. Sometimes I understand your poor father only too well."

"*What!* What do you mean?"

"Only that you're very persistent, and you won't think as you're told. I never understood how annoying that can be."

"Oh."

"Now don't . . ." She looked down, momentarily distracted, as a kitten launched itself onto her skirt and started climbing, with wild eyes and wicked, lashing tail. When it reached her lap, she scooped it up and set it on her shoulder. It was a vivid little calico and looked striking there, beside her white hair and faded face.

"Don't look so crestfallen, Kris," she said. "I may understand him, but I won't be like him any more than I can help—especially now that I know the strength of the temptation."

"Oh."

"Stubbornness is a good thing for a thinker," said Aunt Mil. The kitten's ears leapt forward in excitement. It tapped the corner of her moving mouth. She smiled.

"So come now," she said. "I'm proud of you. It's hard to stand up to someone you love, especially when they're old and overbearing. I'm glad to see you do it. I know you'll never think something you can't believe in, no matter who tells you to. But you mustn't expect it to be comfortable."

Right then I certainly wasn't comfortable. I was aboil with strong emotions: chagrin and self-esteem, explosively mixed; resentment; and love. The trapper was trapped, and the extended family was still the family, where love and manipulation mingled. Not knowing what to say or how to look, I bent to stroke a kitten, thinking, Another reason we have, then—social lubrication.

Aunt Mil's kitten was swinging down from her shoulder, its claws making tiny popping sounds in and out the fabric of her dress. It reached the ground and headed toward the swirl of playing brothers and sisters. Aunt Mil twitched her foot and caught its eye. It came back, to conduct a serious experiment with shoelaces.

"A calico," said Aunt Mil, rather grimly. "Female, of course."

"Robert would like a female better," I said; not quite *to* Aunt Mil but in her direction. "It's better to take a girl. Other people won't."

"Mmm," said Aunt Mil. The calico kitten was mugged by a little tiger. They kicked each other, head and stomach, and squealed in fury.

"This kitten already has a family," she said. "Do we have any right—"

Then she shook her head vigorously. "Oh, don't be foolish! They live with people, and people have power over them. Morally questionable, but that's the way it is. Kris, in the glove compartment you'll find pen and paper. Write a note to your friend, explaining where this kitten's gone."

"But . . ." I said with difficulty. "I don't want to force you. . . ."

"Nonsense, girl, of course you do! What you mean is, you want me not to mind. Well, I don't. The girl who does yard work for me will be cleaning out the litter box, and I shall have all the fun. Now hurry! I want to get her home and see what Robert thinks."

She scooped the kitten up as she finished. Startled and annoyed, it wailed in her face and struggled to get free.

No such luck, kitten! You're in this family now.

THE
SIXTH
SENSE

"**O**H, FOR PETE'S SAKE!" James squeezed his eyes shut for a second, then opened them wide and re-read the sentence in disbelief and horror.

"The instructor is quite right in emphasizing this funda-mental condition for correct locomotion, for without long strides of the hind legs, and hence of the forehand (to which the impulse is communicated through the muscles of the back), no extension is conceivable—"

He snapped the book shut and thrust it back on the shelf, got up restlessly, and stood at the window, hands in pockets.

Rain dripped steadily off the eaves and rippled the broad shallow puddles in the yard. Infrequent gusts of wind blew bright leaves down from the maple. They lay slick and shiny on the brilliant green autumn lawn. It was cold out. James had ridden Ghazal in the covered ring that morning, but he'd elected to give his other horses the day off. Now . . .

Oh, now he was bored. The writer had failed him. He was looking for poetry, for an understanding of the heart, for answers to the questions opening for him ever since the ride on Avatar. The writer gave him "this fundamental condition for correct locomotion."

Bored. He didn't want to go riding, no interesting work to do, no place to go . . .

But he *did* want to ride. He wanted that ideal partnership again. He wanted to go out and work Ghazal through the afternoon, sculpting away all that was not the perfect horse—stiffness, laziness, crookedness, haste.

But Ghazal had earned time off and wouldn't thank him.

Bored. He turned from the window to look at the others in the living room, all reading or knitting.

Bored. He *really* didn't want to ride just to exercise a horse—jingle along some trail to no place in particular. If there was an errand, a destination . . .

Mail a letter? None written.

Carry a message? No reason not to use the phone.

Go look for something? Nothing out there . . . or maybe— yes, he might try again to find the lost military road, which used to lead across their ridge into the next township. Sure, he could do that. A half-assed errand was better than no errand at all.

He put on a sweater and his knee-length, greasy yellow rain poncho. He thought of asking Gloria to come. But no, two people riding through the rain was not the same as one, alone and melancholy, fleeing his own persistent questions.

He slipped out of the house and splashed across the soupy yard to the barn.

Robbie, the young Morgan, was dry in his stall, and James felt guilty taking him out. Perhaps he should give it up. What right did he have to impose his will on a hapless fellow creature?

He settled the question by cinching on the army saddle he used for trail riding, and schooling himself to a rough, no-nonsense attitude. He had the right because he had the power. Robbie spent nine-tenths of his time in the barn, eating his head off. He could go out in the rain once in a while, if his master wished.

Passing under the doorway, Robbie flattened his ears at the first drops and sidled among the puddles as James tried to mount, handicapped by the voluminous poncho. When James swung his leg across, the poncho flapped. Robbie jumped ahead, displaying a rough-and-ready attitude of his own. If James was fool enough to ride out in weather like this, he could take his lumps!

"All right, me boyo!" James muttered. He jammed his foot into the stirrup and booted Robbie ahead, up the woodlot trail.

Normally he liked riding Robbie. Though green, the young horse had a fresh, cheerful forward energy that never needed stoking. Today, though, he was resentful, and James was dreaming of another horse—Avatar, whose power, balance, and educated response made Robbie seem ugly. James found himself consumed with irritation. His temper wasn't helped by the drenchings he got as Robbie scraped him beneath the sodden branches.

He smacked Robbie's neck with his open hand. Robbie

gave a sassy toss of the head. His neck was high and stiff, his trot hard and jouncy. James gritted his teeth. Avatar . . .

He remembered the incredible suppleness, the ease and grace of the great horse. Robbie, by comparison, just chugged along. But Robbie was the natural horse; Avatar was man-made.

That was true, wasn't it? Garry Kunstler had schooled Avatar, developed him from a state of crudeness perhaps similar to Robbie's. The work had shaped his muscles and given him the rounded, distinctive profile of a dressage horse; made him more intelligent; *made* him.

Hast thou given the horse strength? Hast thou clothed his neck with thunder?

Actually, yes. Garry had literally shaped Avatar; and Avatar was on this earth because men had wanted a certain kind of horse on which, in the beginning, to go to war. War had made Avatar, war had made Ghazal, descendant of the ancient military tradition of the Spanish Riding School; war had even made Robbie, whose ancestor, Justin Morgan, was said to be sired by a British officer's mount. War was behind all the million-dollar Arabs, now such a popular hobby with movie-stars. War had made the Great Horses, the declining breeds that once worked the wheat fields. War—all the way back to the runty creatures that pulled the chariots of the Sumerians.

And yet dressage he considered one of the most civilized and peaceable pursuits—

Robbie shied violently at a black stump, which to an excited imagination might conceivably resemble a bear. It was a stump they had passed at least seventy-five times this summer alone. James bit down on his annoyance and concentrated on the familiar trail.

The Sixth Sense

It intersected the military road in the fern-filled corner of a stone wall, two miles from the house. All that way Robbie's protest continued unabated. Not by chance was James dragged beneath so many low, sodden branches. The hood of his poncho hung heavy down his back like a water balloon and sloshed with Robbie's every jiggle. Cold water thrilled down his back; water dripped steadily off his visor. His fingers were chilled on the slippery reins.

He paused in the belly-deep ferns, burned gold and brown by frost, and looked uphill, where the faint track disappeared in ledge and fallen leaves.

This is stupid, horse! His hands tightened on the reins. He thought he'd turn around.

But the wet leather slid through his fingers, and Robbie, determined to be naughty, forged ahead through the ferns. The tips slapped James's knees, soaking his jeans in the small space between poncho and boot top. He gave way to the adventure, to the odd pleasure of persisting in foolishness.

This ride belonged to another tradition of horsemanship— the messenger, the traveler, the cowboy—users of horses for pragmatic human purposes, hired hands on horseback, riders in the rain. It was a tradition that left the horse mostly to himself, trusting in his native sense and surefootedness; a tradition that cared little for purity of gait, beauty, or exactitude, as long as the horse covered ground.

A saner tradition, maybe, thought James as Robbie scrambled up the rocky ridge, slippery with wet leaves. He bowed low to Robbie's neck, and the branches scraped across his back. He smelled hot, damp horse.

What does a horse care if it makes a round circle instead of an oval? They just want to eat and wander. Why should we fiddle with their minds?

Yet automatically, as Robbie reached the piny top of the ridge and began to trot, James made him go straight and pushed him up to take frank contact with the bit. He gazed morosely at the nervous little ears, flicking back toward him in cursory attention, then snapping forward as Robbie's thoughts fastened on the trail ahead. In cowboy tradition he should let the reins slop now, and relax his driving legs. Just travel, never mind how. He knew he wouldn't, for the result would be intolerably ugly.

Why wasn't plain traveling enough? It had its own beauty. It was no stranger to balance and rhythm.

But there was nowhere to go. No one's life was so constructed that a horse could take them anyplace essential. No important work was done on horseback. When people went trail riding now, it was just play, and if that was all there was to riding, he would be in college now. He saw himself, loafers, chinos, and yellow sweater, feet firmly on the path to business school, dollar signs for eyes. Shiver.

Shiver. Cold day! He sniffed at a drop on the end of his nose, which was only water and made him sneeze. Then Robbie hesitated under him, and looking up, he saw that they'd come to the end.

Here the big ridge they'd been following disappeared, forking and forking again into a dozen high, rocky ridgelets with deep ravines between. Here was where he and every Mac-Liesh before him had begun to get lost.

He made Robbie stand, requiring a good, four-cornered halt. Slowly and thoughtfully he looked down every ravine and along every ridge top, considered the age of every tree, and tried to decide where he would put a military road if he were General John Stark on his way to Fort Crown Point.

I sure as heck wouldn't put it here!

He turned in the saddle softly, to keep Robbie still, and looked back. It was possible they'd always come too far, that the trail angled off at some earlier point, and that already he was lost.

Yet he didn't think so. The way behind him led straight and clear to Robbie's hind feet. The military road must take one of these ravines, one of these ridge tops. Which?

Robbie bobbed his nose impatiently and took a couple of unbidden steps, choosing the ravine straight ahead. That was the one they'd taken last time, that looked so plain and ended a hundred yards downhill in a tangle of spruce.

Come to think of it, they'd always tried ravines, never ridges. The ridges were steep and treacherous; bare exposed rock and slippery leaves, roots writhing over the surface like snakes hunting a hole. . . .

But to the left was a ridge with a broad, flat top, nearly as passable as the big ridge that had just ended. Men could march along it if the trees were cleared. A horse could make his way even now. No other ridge was so broad; no other seemed possible. James made his choice.

Still, he wasn't confident. He put Robbie up what had seemed a gradual slope, and felt the horse's withers rise steeply before him, his hooves slip and scramble. His breath made big clouds of steam through which they passed. Saplings on either side constantly menaced James's knees. Only his quick reflexes saved him from a crushing.

When they reached the level area, it was less level than it had seemed, and narrower. James viewed it dubiously, wishing he knew his history better. How big was a Colonial army? How would they have marched? Might they have split up here? Flowed through all the ravines and over all the ridges, to regroup on the other side?

Good questions. He kept going because he didn't see a better choice.

Robbie stepped unwarily into a leaf-filled hollow, jolted and snorted. "C'mon, Rob, watch where you're goin'!" He listened with his body for a few strides, trying to feel out any lameness. None, apparently. Robbie was no good for a job like this. Too hasty, too jumpy, mind anywhere but his feet. For going like this you wanted a sage, mature—

Blow from the side! Branches clawed his face; his foot was torn from the stirrup. The bright leaves smeared and slid and spun around him . . . wet slaps in the face. He hauled Robbie to a standstill, gasping, trying to realize what had happened.

Bashed me on a tree.

"You do that on purpose, little bastard?"

The sick, stunned feeling drained slowly. Robbie fidgeted, and somewhat vindictively James snatched him up short. "Stand, damn you!" He started to grope for his lost stirrup.

"*Ouch!*"

His knee hurt. Cautiously he moved it and had to bite his lip at the sudden pain. Broken? Torn cartilage? "Robbie, I could *kill* you!"

Holding Robbie on a very tight rein, he bent and gently probed with his fingers, then massaged more deeply, wiggled the kneecap. The pain didn't get any worse. Just bruised, he thought with a sigh of relief.

The stirrup was gone.

"Oh, hell." He looked back and saw it lying in the leaves many feet behind him. It had torn from the safety bar as a stirrup is supposed to, to save a rider from being dragged. James said a number of unkind things to Robbie, turned him, and rode back to it.

He dismounted, lighting gingerly on his hurt leg, slid the stirrup leather back over the safety bar, and looked around, reassessing his position.

The ridge dropped steeply down before him, disappearing in deep golden ferns. Many yards away, it curved up again, undulating through the woods like a sea serpent. On either side the undergrowth looked impassable.

He looked at the slope again and sighed. Too steep to ride down, with Robbie acting like this. Have to lead him.

"All right, here we go. *Be careful,* you little jerk!"

Robbie had no intention of being careful. His eyes glowed, his breath came in great puffs, his feet scattered recklessly on the leaves. James had to brace against him at every step, which did his knee no good.

"Whoa, Robbie!" He wished he had a different horse. Even Petra, who threw herself over backward, had some sense on the trail.

Despite everything, they reached the bottom safely. James mounted and found he couldn't flex his knee enough to find the stirrup. He rode up the next ridge, bushwhacked across the top, dismounted, and slid down the other side.

His knee hurt too much for this. Next time the ridge dipped down, he stayed in the saddle. It felt perilous; himself so high in the air, Robbie's withers falling away in front of him, all the scrabbling, scraping sounds from the four hooves so far below. But they got safely to the bottom. Robbie's third ridge; he was beginning to know how to handle them.

Now a broad, ferny corridor opened up, running parallel to

the spine of rock they followed. James turned into it, grateful for the respite.

He listened to the quiet, dripping woods, and Robbie's footfalls so loud in it. He already felt a long way from home, but at least it seemed he'd been on the right track. This corridor made easy riding, and his imagination filled it with an army of men in buckskins, marching shoulder to shoulder. Beside and in front rode officers. . . .

Officers. Again his mind slipped into the well-worn groove; the Spanish Riding School in Vienna and the school at Saumer, and beyond. The Mongols, the Slavic riders on the plains of Eastern Europe, knights on Great Horses, Arabs in a swirl of robes, Athenians in the time of Xenophon, twenty-three centuries past.

He, in America, was a very late follower in this procession. He tried to place himself precisely; Vermont, somewhere between two townships, late twentieth century; of the educated upper class, though not educated or upper himself; on a horse bred to work small hill-farms and amuse country people in harness racing. He did not ride to kill anyone, defend any civilization, or prove any point. Robbie would never clear a field or carry a family to town in a farm wagon. The traditions they belonged to were old and cold. The trail they followed was cold, too, built by dead men to take them to a dead fort, for reasons James could not clearly recall.

Then why? Why do this?

Why follow this trail? Why keep breeding Morgan horses? Especially, why learn and practice the discipline of the European riding schools, the outgrown relic of a dead way of warfare?

Was it only a game? Elaborate cowboys and Indians?

He didn't care for that idea. What he did felt more essential than that—something necessary, something from the core.

I suppose I'm bred to ride, he thought, as much as they're bred to be ridden. Throughout history the riders had been the winners and the survivors, stamping the gene pool with their type. Perhaps it was by deepest instinct that so many little children cantered so joyfully, champing imaginary bits, hands on imaginary reins—the original centaurs. To be part horse, an ancient human dream. Imagine! A little Mongol child, a little Arab, a little Greek . . .

He suggested that Robbie trot, here where the going was so fine, and began to think about dressage, the most self-disciplining of these ancient paths. To do dressage was also to be a centaur, to be so much a part of a horse that you placed him precisely where you wanted, at precisely the correct moment. It was control, down to the very stride—every stride. And it was freedom; the horse freely assenting to the control, with relaxed muscles and with glad cooperation. Horse and rider both must be gay and bold and buoyant, thoughtful, controlled, and exact. It was this paradox that made dressage such a pleasure of the mind. The rest of life should be like that. . . .

He came around a bend, and his fine corridor disappeared. A thick wall of spruce grew up before him, and beyond them he could make out a steep slope strewn with chunks of granite and thickly grown with trees.

Robbie turned around matter-of-factly, and headed back the way he'd come.

"Oh no, you don't! We have to climb again."

The ridge was more fractured here, brushier, slick with wet leaves, confusing. Promising pathways ended in steep drops or in thickets, and they had to retrace their steps. It seemed to James that Robbie was always going a shade too fast. While his own eyes searched for a safe way, Robbie was moving on a slight tangent and getting them into trouble.

They scraped through dripping branches, slipped on leafy slopes, stumbled over tangles of downed trees. Once Robbie tripped getting over a heap of loose stone and almost fell from under James. He scrambled forward to regain his balance and then stopped, jammed against some saplings. James let him stand and breathe, rubbing his own knee, which had been wrenched in the stumble. The pain was swelling, hot and sick.

After a moment he noticed that Robbie's breath still came quick and agitated. He laid his hand on the young horse's shoulder and felt him tremble.

"What's the matter, Rob? Hurt yourself?"

He couldn't dismount here. They were too close to the saplings on one side, and on the other the rock sloped down sharply. He urged Robbie a few steps onward, to a more open and level spot, listening intently with his body for any lameness. He felt nothing.

Slowly and stiffly he dismounted. He was beginning to think more seriously now that this was a foolish enterprise—risking the legs of his good young horse, risking his own knee . . . knees are nothing to fool around with.

He stooped, running a hand down each hard black leg. No swelling, no scratches. But Robbie still seemed deeply agitated, a state far different from his earlier spooks and naughtiness. The fall had scared him.

Scared me, too, thought James. He stood with his hand on Robbie's quivering neck, looking around. This wild tangle of brush and broken rock was not a trail. He should have seen that at once. He should have resisted the blind urge to go forward, when there was no obvious way.

"Anyway, little fella, let's get you down off this rock."

It was easier said than done, but after limping along a little farther, James found a path. He had to go down on the opposite side from the ferny corridor, which made him uneasy. His thoughts were becoming disorganized. Time to turn around, before he got lost.

But when he reached the level, a new path seemed to open up paralleling the ridge, and he thought, One more try. He checked the girth and gathered the reins to mount. Reaching for the pommel, he saw across the back of his right hand a thick smear of blood.

His heart thudded. Blood didn't make him queasy, but alone here in the dripping woods, it had a powerful, primitive effect. He found himself listening hard.

After a second he collected himself and stepped back a couple of paces, looking at Robbie. He saw no hurt, but Robbie still seemed upset and sorry for himself.

Something must be wrong! Blood doesn't come from nowhere. Me? He ran a quick inventory and found himself intact.

He stepped to Robbie's head and stroked him, speaking softly, trying to think. The blood, now thinned by rainwater, filled his eyes. . . .

And now there was more, smeared on his yellow poncho where Robbie's nose had rested. James gripped the cheekpiece and bent to look at Robbie's muzzle. Then he turned away, feeling sick.

No, it couldn't be as bad as that. He looked again.

All right, it's not that bad. Just the end of Robbie's wiggly, expressive upper lip, bashed on the rock. Bruise and contusion, raw patch of flesh the size of a quarter . . .

He could not continue the assessment. The shock to his own nerves was almost as great as that to Robbie's. He straightened queasily and rubbed the little horse's neck.

"All right, that's it. Let's go home."

He wasn't going to attempt the ridge again. He set off along its base, leading Robbie. The trees grew thick on all sides, and the footing was rough. Limping, James chose the easiest path, though it led in slightly the wrong direction. Somewhere soon he would see a place to turn.

It wasn't actually a path, just a series of relatively open spaces between the trees and undergrowth that drew the eye. A serpentine progression; so many yards in one direction, so many in another; stop, look, and turn again. He tried always to keep the gray spine of the ridge in view, but after one complicated series of zigzags, he looked and it was gone.

He stopped, gazing back beyond Robbie's haunches. Already he was a little unsure of the way they'd come. Should he try to retrace his steps or go on?

Go on, he supposed. Here under the trees, the afternoon was already darkening toward night; he would have turned back soon, even if he had found the trail. He thought he was heading in roughly the right direction. Soon he would hit the ridge again, or come out someplace familiar.

Robbie followed docilely. He was tired and upset, and seemed to draw reassurance from James. It hardly made sense. James was the one who had dragged him from his dry stall, forced him over rough country, and gotten him hurt. James wasn't even sure where they were anymore.

"Quit it!" he said when Robbie reached forward to nudge

him confidingly in the back. "You don't know anything, horse!"

The ridge did not reappear. A series of fallen hemlocks and ambitious young thickets drove them gradually downhill. Shooting pains began to radiate from James's knee. His legs were soaked. His nose dripped. Wind shook a shower of droplets from the tree branches. When the wind stopped, the shower went on. It was possible to get wetter.

Nobody knows where I am, he thought, remembering how quietly he had slipped out of the house. They wouldn't miss him till chore time, and then there was nothing they could do.

Curious, how unsettling it seemed to be incommunicado. It added an extra thrill to the sensation of being lost—

Not lost! he told himself quickly. Mislaid. He would not be lost—he wouldn't *feel* lost—while he still had Robbie's company.

Instantly his imagination supplied a new scenario; Robbie breaking loose and galloping away, leaving him alone. Robbie arriving at the barn door with broken reins and scarred saddle, hungry for his supper.

Robbie, arriving at the barn door!

He stopped and looked hard at his little horse; the careless, silly young animal with the bashed lip and trusting expression. "Do *you* know the way?"

It was often so in stories, the sagacious horse taking the hero home; the lost hero, the wounded hero. James had accepted it as a romantic convention. He didn't really believe in the mysterious sixth sense, the supposed inner compass possessed by animals. After all, *he* was an animal, and he'd never felt it. It was notably absent in the present circumstances.

Still, worth a try.

He stepped back to Robbie's side, leaving the reins slack. "Go on, boy! Go home!"

Robbie turned curiously to face him. James stepped back again. Robbie turned. They made a full circle.

No good. Robbie was obviously depending on him, which meant the inner compass hadn't a clue. James started to walk again. He wondered if he was destroying his knee.

Maybe if he mounted and just sat there, Robbie would take the initiative.

It was hard to mount. His legs were stiff and tired, and the soaked jeans stuck to his skin. But it felt wonderful to take the weight off his knee and rest. He let the reins hang in long loops. When Robbie didn't move, he urged him gently. "Go on, Rob."

Robbie stepped off tentatively. At first he seemed to do as James had, choosing the open places and the easy going, wandering at random. He had no concept of James's extra height above him. James had to stay alert, ready to fling himself on Robbie's neck whenever a low branch came at him. He was scraped and soaked and stabbed with twigs. Rain pattered on his slicker.

Gradually, though, he began to sense a trend to Robbie's wandering. It seemed wrong; surely they should be heading more toward the east?

Or was this east? Without the sun for guidance, all directions looked the same. The day was completely gray around him; gray sky, gray mist, lit by a flame of maple or golden, frost-touched fern, but no sun. The moss grew all around the tree trunks. Perhaps it was thickest on the north side, but James couldn't tell from the saddle, didn't think enough of the theory to bother dismounting.

The Sixth Sense

All at once Robbie stopped short. He tossed his head up, testing the air, and then a tremendous neigh shook his body. He started to trot. James fell onto his neck as the dimly seen branches leapt back at him.

It seemed they were on a trail. Lying on Robbie's neck, he sometimes saw what looked like bare, packed dirt; but in the dusk he couldn't be sure.

Robbie stopped again and dropped his head, nearly shooting James out of the saddle. His breath came in loud, excited puffs—sniffing something. Peering down the dim sweep of Robbie's neck, James discerned a shadowy mound of horse manure.

They *were* on a trail!

Having gleaned all available information from this heap, Robbie trotted on. He kept his head low and stopped often, apparently smelling other piles of manure. James could no longer make them out. He held tightly to Robbie's mane against the jolting stops and kept his head down, for it was too dark to see the branches.

Once more Robbie paused, then gave a loud neigh with an excited blast of breath at the end. Then he listened, so still that the beat of his heart moved James in the saddle. James listened also, thought he heard a faraway whinny. Robbie's body seemed to settle in relief. He started off again.

He seemed to have forgotten that he bore a rider. His step had the power and spring of a stallion at liberty. To James, it was like riding a trained dressage horse in light collection, a little like riding Avatar.

For a moment, in the pleasure of the motion beneath him, he forgot he was lost. This was as fine as anything he'd ever gotten from a horse, and Robbie was doing it all by himself.

An earlier paradox popped back into his head. If Avatar was man-made, then how *could* Robbie do this, all by himself?

Answer, of course—Avatar was not man-made. He was man-enhanced. His movements were nothing that was not natural for a horse . . . but a horse left alone would not naturally do them. Avatar was, in fact, more natural than a natural horse. . . .

And James, who had ridden a long way to escape questions such as these, had found them waiting for him at the edge of the woods. He grinned at himself. Up ahead, now, he saw gray light through the trees.

Robbie accelerated, slipping a little on the wet leaves. They broke out of the woods at the top of a long slope, and James found himself staring down at a strange house and barn.

He straightened from his crouch and made Robbie stand, filled with unreasoning disappointment. So much for the good old sixth sense! Where were they? He supposed he'd have to ride down and ask. . . .

Robbie jerked the reins impatiently, neighing. Close at hand, an answer came out of the darkness, and James heard the thud of trotting hooves. Shadowy horses approached. Some distance away they stopped, milling. He could just make out a line of fence posts.

A sudden light flared down in the yard. The kitchen door opened, and a man stood there, looking up the hill—a familiar man, in a red-and-black plaid jacket. He was the professor and breeder from whom James had bought Robbie over a year and a half ago.

He stood looking up toward his horses a minute, then seemed to see James. The shiny yellow slicker must stand out brilliantly against the black hill and the black woods. The professor lifted one hand in calm salute.

Robbie shifted under James, almost unseen. Little horse. James touched his neck, apologizing. In his mind's eye he saw Robbie, silly, mischievous colt, hunting his way along the dark trails; keen, nervous, still unsure in his ancient animal understanding; making his way back here, to the place where he was born. Little Robbie . . .

A gust of wind drove the rain rattling against the slicker; cold on James's face. He raised a hand in belated answer to the professor's wave and pointed Robbie down across the field on a long diagonal, toward the gate and the trail home.

THEA

"Here, Thea!" Phillip called. "Here, Thea! *Thea!*"

Thea sat in the center of his bedroom rug with her white paws primly side by side, blinking up at his face. The impression she conveyed was of a cat who knew exactly what was going on; who held him in tolerant affection but wasn't going to jump through hoops for him.

He rattled the cardboard container of cat treats. Her pupils jumped wide for a second, but she only adjusted her paws and purred audibly at him across the room.

"Oh, for heaven's sake!" Phillip cried. She was making him feel like a fool. He went across to where she sat and gave her a treat. She ate it with dainty satisfaction, then rubbed around his legs approvingly.

"Hey! Who's training who here?"

"*Mee,*" said Thea.

"Yeah, you! You're a witch, that's what you are!" He picked her up and lay across the bed. Thea arranged herself on his chest, paws tucked under her breastbone. She beamed down into his face, purring so heartily that he felt the vibration through all his internal organs. Once again he felt he'd done just what she wanted.

"You know what I think?" he said. "I think you cats are an alien race, taking us over by mind power. You make us your slaves, and you make us like it. The human race is doomed!" At the moment he did feel taken over, with Thea's purr humming within him and the condescending looks of approval she cast him from time to time. Poor nice dumb slave Phillip! A pat on the head will make him feel good.

"You treat us like dogs," he said.

Dogs could be bought with a little approval. Dogs could be bullied. Dogs could be trained. Dogs were smothery, and slobbered affection on you at inconvenient moments. Rebuke them and they lay around looking sad and sighing. Dogs were heavy.

Pigs, now . . . actually he preferred not to think about pigs. He considered other farm animals as he had known them. Cows were vague, stubborn, and seemed unrelated to people. Cows and people treated each other as objects, and obstacles. The relationship, on both sides, was conducted on a level of low cunning . . . except that cows were innocent, however annoying; like crying babies. Humans were not.

Goats were different, now. His two aunts, Vivian and Pat,

kept goats, and it seemed almost like they lived in a commune. The goats weren't pets, they weren't spoken of like children; but they weren't just livestock, either. They were more like partners, and Vivian mentioned them casually in her letters—Amy, Leah, Tony. . . .

The neighbor's motorcycle roared to life, tearing apart the quiet afternoon. Thea jumped, sat up on Phillip's chest looking annoyed, and then soothed herself with a bath. The motorcycle revved for several minutes before the neighbor departed, trailing the sound a long way behind him. Phillip clenched tight fistfuls of the bedspread. "Bastard, I hate your guts!" he whispered. Why should people have so much power to ruin other people's quiet? *Damn* it. . . .

Thea glanced up suddenly from her laundry, and a second later Phillip heard a girl's voice. "This is the house."

Go away, he thought. Shut up and go away!

"It doesn't look like anyone's home," said another voice— an older woman. Burglars, casing the joint? Jehovah's Witnesses?

"I'd like to see the girl, anyway," the younger voice said wistfully. "Greg's gone *bananas* over her."

Greg would be one of the half dozen boys who whirred up their dead-end street on bikes all day long, hoping for a glimpse of Carrie. They looked to be his own age. They probably didn't know that Carrie was three years older and going to nursing school in the fall. Phillip had marked them down on his mental list of people not to make friends with.

"Oh, look! Chicks!" the old lady cried. "I should have thought keeping chickens would be illegal in this part of town."

"*Everything* interesting's illegal in this part of town," the girl said bitterly.

Well, now, a girl after his own heart! Ruthlessly he dumped Thea to the floor, swiveled on his bed, and peeked out the narrow crack between the edge of the curtain and the window frame.

Out in the sunny street, looking over the picket fence into the yard, stood a tall, straight girl in jeans, and a taller, straighter old lady in a denim jumper. No Bibles, but both had a fanatical look about the mouth, a look of intolerance.

"Chickens are disgusting things," said the woman, after they had watched the baby chicks a few minutes.

"Why?"

"Oh, the way they peck at one another. If one is hurt, showing a little blood, or it looks the least bit different, they'll all gang up and peck the poor thing to death. Makes you ashamed."

"Ashamed?" The girl looked, frowning, from her grandmother to the baby chicks. At last her expression lightened, and she shook her head decisively.

"No. Now you sound like Dad."

"How so?"

"Oh, he loves to do that—point out something that animals do that seems vicious, and . . . and . . . uh . . ."

The old lady had made some mental leap and now looked perfectly enlightened, but she let the girl struggle on.

"Well, he somehow makes out from that that the world is basically bad, that people can't help the terrible things they do, and we might as well not even try. And I hate it!"

"Hmm," said the old lady thoughtfully. "Deriving a moral principle from animal behavior—that's quite sentimental thinking, Kris." The idea appeared to give her satisfaction.

Then she looked at the chicks again, and the satisfaction disappeared. "On the other hand—"

"Oh, look!" the girl interrupted, pointing at Phillip's window.

Phillip jerked back from the curtain and flattened against the wall, heart beating rapidly. I won't answer the door, he thought. No one's home. . . .

"Her name is Thea," said the girl. "Isn't she neat?"

"Oh, yes, she's somebody!"

Phillip relaxed against his wall. Thea stood with hind paws still on his bed and front paws on the windowsill, her body stretched long across the gulf.

"Show-off!" he hissed. Ignoring him, Thea got gracefully onto the windowsill and settled herself, like a queen granting audience. She was purring.

"My, she's quite a little minx!" said the old lady.

"Hi, Thea," called the girl. "Remember me?"

Wait a minute! thought Phillip. How does she know Thea's name? He risked another furtive peep but had to duck back too quickly. She did look familiar.

"Well, we shouldn't hang around too long," said the girl when they had admired Thea some more. "What if they come home?"

"I thought that was the whole idea."

"No-ooo! Aunt *Mil*!"

"Sorry. I misunderstood. . . ." The voices were starting to recede. Phillip came boldly to the window, watching the two straight backs disappear up the street. They were talking again. What had the old lady been about to say when she was interrupted? On the other hand . . .

The girl made a wide gesture as she disappeared beyond the third house down. What on earth were they talking about?

"No, Thea, you can't come." He ducked out his bedroom

door and shut it quickly in Thea's face; out the kitchen door, down the driveway, stopping at the end, and watching the two high heads until they turned the corner. Then he sprinted after them. Please, nobody see me doing this. Nobody's looking out their window . . .

When he reached the corner, the two figures had disappeared.

Phillip shoved his hands in his pockets and began walking rapidly, glancing down the side streets as he passed, whistling. He spotted his quarry in the third street and turned down it, slowing his gait to a shamble, looking innocently into front yards. The girl and old lady turned in at a hedge and a red mailbox, and he remembered—a half-seen girl sitting on the steps, Thea running toward him. "Don't be taken in," she had said.

Just for the looks of it, he loitered down to the end of the street, which dropped off like their own in a steep, eroding sandbank, down to the river. There he stood, watching the broad, murky, undramatic flow. How do I get to know them? he wondered. How do I find out what they're *talking* about?

He thought of a way, but by the time his chance came, he was almost too angry to use it.

It was Friday night. They were going to the mall with some of the new friends his mother had made so easily, and Phillip had refused to come along.

"Phillip's being difficult," his mother said at last to the other woman. She laughed to show it didn't matter, but Phillip heard the angry edge to her voice.

"Well," said the other woman heartily, "all teenagers rebel. Comes with the territory."

Oh, *Christ*! Phillip swung away to stare out the window, blowing his breath out audibly.

Carrie gave him a wink as she hitched her pocketbook strap up onto her shoulder. She was last out the door, and before she shut it, she called in softly, "So long, rebel. Don't play with matches!"

Carrie understood, but she was still going to spend the evening at the mall.

He stood at the window watching them arrange themselves in the car; the other man driving, with his father in the front seat, the three women in the back. His father's chest looked sunken, as if it had been hollow all along and a sudden blow had caved it in. Phillip wondered if that was real, or only his imagination. He'd heard his mother say hysterically, "His lungs are just *gone*!"

A man whose lungs were gone, a family uprooted, four whole lives changed forever, and all they could think to do was go to the mall!

He went out on the cement front steps, to look bitterly at the houses on either side and across the street. Each had a picture window. Through each picture window he saw the pale flicker of a television. Everybody's garbage can was set out by the mailbox. Everybody's driveway held a nice newish, middling-expensive car. Phillip's stomach convulsed with hatred.

He turned around quickly and went inside, thinking, Thoreau complained about Concord, but he never saw *this*! Everything conventional, mass-produced, and ugly. Every house on this street was made to the same plan. The only thing allowed to differ was the shade of paint.

Get hold of yourself, rebel! The farm wasn't heaven.

No, the farm was hell. The hog pens were built over manure pits. The barn kept the fumes inside until they reached toxic levels, but that never affected the hogs, for they didn't live long enough to get sick. They were farrowed and fattened and slaughtered, the span of their lives measured in weeks. His father, with a longer exposure to the fumes and to pesticides, herbicides, antibiotic dusts, and tobacco smoke, was the one who'd gotten sick; he and the barn cats, who were always dying mysterious early deaths.

The farm was ugly and it stank, but at least it had some texture. At least people worked there, did real and necessary things. You could walk to someplace beautiful—the creek where wild plums grew, the cottonwood bluff. He would rather live there than here, where everything was packaged just the same. The only thing that marked his family as different from any other was the chicken yard, which was probably illegal.

Then he remembered the girl and her old aunt, and he remembered his plan.

Still, he almost didn't. He went toward his room, thrashing in his angry thoughts like a man in quicksand and only sinking deeper. Of *course* we rebel, he was thinking. We're smart enough to want something better, and not old enough to get it. There's nowhere for me, no place where . . .

Thea met him, curving herself around the corner of his door with a thin cry. Thea, the last barn cat.

Phillip watched as she strolled down the short hall to her food dish, gave it a passing glance, and leapt onto the sink to look out the window. There were birds in the yard. Her tail began to twitch, like an extension of her calculating brain. She looked the embodiment of evil, crouching there, intent on the kill. *Could* an animal be evil? Anyway, he was glad to be larger than Thea, and hence her friend. He remembered the old lady: "Chickens are disgusting things!"

All right.

He scooped Thea up, closing one hand firmly across her breast to prevent sudden leaps, and went out the door. He thought he should be locking up but didn't bother. He walked down the dusky street, silent in his sneakers; past the mailboxes and the mid-size cars, past the picture windows and the leaping blue light. He turned the corner, walked three streets up, and turned again.

"Okay, Thea, go right where you went before, remember? Remember that girl?"

Thea wasn't listening. She sat bolt upright in Phillip's arms, her clear eyes huge and glowing. She was beautiful; the only beautiful thing in his life, Phillip thought.

They were nearing the house with the red mailbox. Phillip's heart began to thump a little. He was glad of the hedge. He would stop at the end of it, put Thea down in the driveway—

A black-and-tan terrier lunged out of the yard he was passing, with a belligerent whoof. Thea shot out of his arms, landed ten feet away on the pavement, and raced across the opposite lawn, her tail as big around as her body, and the terrier in yapping pursuit. They disappeared.

For a second Phillip stood blank. Then he sprinted after them, under a TV-lit picture window, across a neat clipped lawn, along a picket fence, always guided by the barks. *"Dog!"* he yelled. *"Dog!* Quit it! *Thea!"*

Yard lights snapped on. A man's voice shouted aggressively, "What's going on out there?"

"I lost my cat!" Phillip shouted back. He didn't want the guy calling the cops. *"Dog! Quit* that!"

The dog and Thea were at least two backyards away, receding. How could they go so fast when neither of them came as high as his knee? He vaulted over someone's low hedge and landed on someone's little red wagon. It flipped, catching him behind the knees, and he nearly went down. "The-*a!*" Now they were three more yards away, and across the street. He hurdled the hedge at the other side of the lawn as a yard light came on behind him and a voice shouted, *"Hey!"*

Across the street, the dog stopped barking.

Phillip ran as straight as he could remember, toward where he'd last heard the noise. His breath seared down his chest. He was out of shape from lying too much on his bed and hating.

Why did the dog stop barking? Did he catch Thea and shake her? Was she dead?

His feet made two sharp slaps on the pavement, and then he was across the street in someone else's yard. There he stopped, trying to gulp down each breath as it came whistling out; trying to listen.

At first all he heard were voices from a television set, in the small, unsuspecting house near which he stood. When he managed to filter that out of his consciousness, he became aware of a whoofling, sniffing noise, coming from the next-door backyard. He pushed through the hedge.

The dog ran in widening circles with its nose to the close-shaved lawn, obviously trying to pick up a trail. Thea was nowhere in sight.

"Phew!" The dog gave him a passing glance as it continued casting about for a scent. Phillip considered kicking it.

Now, where was Thea?

A voice down the street called, *"Alex! Here, Alex!"* The dog pricked its ears, listening, then shot away, around the corner of the house and down the street. Phillip heard the scratch of its claws on the blacktop, and the jangle of tags. Alex! Obnoxious name for an obnoxious little cur!

"Thea," he called very softly. "Thea."

A fresh fear roosted on his heart. Thea didn't know this place. They'd been keeping her in the house; to acclimate her, to keep her safe from cars and neighborhood dogs. What if she got lost? With all this pavement and mowed-off lawns, and nothing to distinguish one house from another, how could she ever find them again?

"Thea?" he called. The louder cry released more desperation in him. Next time he yelled. *"Thea!"*

A woman's round face looked out the window, showing consternation. She seemed unable to see him.

"I'm looking for my cat," he called to her. All this shouting was doing him no good. It was shaking things loose inside. Now, not so deep down, he felt himself crying. It was only a matter of time before that worked to the surface. He turned away from the house, whispering, *"Thea!"*

A screen door fell shut on the other side of the house— someone coming out. Go away, Phillip thought. Just go away!

"Hello. Can I help you find her?"

It was the girl. In the grid of light from the kitchen window, she looked tall and straight and strong. She looked good to him. He hated her.

It's not worth it. If I've got to lose Thea, it isn't worth it.

"There was a dog," he said. "I caught up to it here, sniffing around . . ."

"Then she's probably close. Up a tree, I bet. I'll get a flashlight."

Thea

This side of the lot was bordered by tall white pines, ten or twelve all in a row. Perhaps they had been planted in ignorance, by someone who thought they would make a hedge. Now they stood up strong against the sky, bigger and wilder than anything in the neighborhood. Beneath them, a thick carpet of fallen needles had conquered the lawn. Phillip walked softly up and down, listening. It made sense that Thea would have climbed a tree. He hoped it was true, and not a time-wasting diversion.

The girl came back with two flashlights. She gave him one and walked away to the other end of the row. Phillip was glad she wasted no time in talk.

The flashlight beam would not penetrate far into the soft green masses above. By raising his arm straight in the air, like the Statue of Liberty with her torch, Phillip could make it go farther, but not more than halfway. How high would Thea climb? He walked all around the first tree, all around the second.

"Should you call?" asked the girl.

Yes, he should, and perhaps he could, now that he'd had a few quiet minutes to himself. "Thea! Thea?"

"Did you hear that?" the girl asked quickly.

"I think it was just a branch. Thea?"

Again a small squeak penetrated the black silence. It seemed to come from the center of the row of trees. Phillip hurried toward the spot, flashlight high. "Thea?"

"*Mee!*"

The beam flashed across something. Phillip brought it back swiftly, to strike squarely on Thea's broad white tuxedo front.

She sat complacently on a large limb, nearly out of flash-light range, white paws neatly tucked together. When the beam shone on her, she uttered another thin, high-pitched comment, narrowing her eyes against the light. She sounded as if she were in her own house, inquiring about supper. But when Phillip lowered the beam a little, it showed a huge, fluffed-out tail hanging off the other side of the branch. The very tip of the tail crooked back and forth, back and forth.

"Come down!" Phillip called. "It's safe now. He's gone."

Thea uttered a long, thin comment that sounded like, "*Naah!*" She was doing fine just where she was.

"She won't come down for at least half an hour," the girl said confidently.

How do you know so much? Phillip wondered. He folded himself cross-legged onto the bed of pine needles.

"I'll just sit here and wait," he said. "Uh—thanks for the help."

"Oh, no problem. You keep the flashlight till tomorrow. I'll come over and get it."

"Oh." Phillip had forgotten the flashlight. "Hey!" he called as the girl started around the corner of the garage. "Thanks a lot! I really mean it—I might never have found her without your help."

"She'd have been all right," the girl said, twirling, but not stopping or slowing down. "Thea's cool."

Phillip heard the screen door bang, and a woman's voice anxiously start asking questions. Not the old lady—what was her name? Aunt Mil.

He flicked the flashlight on for a second, to shine on the two white semicircles of toes on the limb above. "Hey, you! Come on down now!" He got another negative comment.

Funny, he thought, turning off the flashlight; funny that

they each knew something they weren't telling. She knew where he lived. He knew she'd come over that day. She knew Thea's name. He knew her aunt's. He liked it that way. That was fine.

He relaxed there in the quiet. The residue of his panic seemed to run out of him and sink into the earth. He liked being a stranger in this neighborhood; the only person outdoors, the only person sitting quietly, not watching a television. No one knew he was here but the girl and Thea.

Thea spoke to him from her branch, several times. When at last he got tired and stopped answering, she began to move around. He pointed the flashlight and watched her delicate maneuverings. How precisely she dropped from one limb to another! Her paws landed just where they should, never slipping. Then she hesitated and looked carefully, chose the next limb, and figured out how to get to it. She was small, serious, and absorbed, for the moment paying him no attention.

When she reached the last limb, she paused. Then she uttered a small worried cry—talking to herself, not Phillip—and swung out onto the trunk, grappling with her claws. Her ears were laid back in concentration, yet she lowered herself with the confidence and skill of a steeplejack.

Phillip stood and, as she came within his reach, took hold of her. She stiffened against him, clinging to the bark, until he stroked her. Then her purr started, very loud in the quiet night, and she slashed him nearly to ribbons, twisting in his hands and clawing up onto his shoulder. The purr was thunderous in his ears, such a mighty purr that she choked from time to time and had to swallow and begin again.

He took a firm hold on her tail, in case she jumped again, and he walked around the garage and onto the street, saying goodbye silently to the picture window leaping with blue television light. He walked home. The dog did not jump out again, and the house had not been burglarized, in all this time that it had been left unlocked. His family was not yet home from the mall.

He awoke late the next morning. Thea was gone from his pillow, but he could see the round indentation where she had slept all night, close to his head. He glanced at his alarm clock, got up, and dressed quickly. What time would the girl come over for her flashlight? If she liked him, she might come early.

He stepped out into the hall and heard his mother crying in the kitchen. His stomach clutched in a hard knot, and he looked into his parents' bedroom. There lay his father, in his striped pajamas, snoring as loudly as if his lungs were whole. Phillip knew himself to be relieved, but his stomach stayed knotted as he went out to the kitchen.

His mother sat at the table with a box of tissues beside her. Methodical and tidy in everything, she had settled down for a good cry. Phillip could have smiled, except that her shoulders shook so hard; and her face, when she looked up at him, was so pale and slack. He stayed across the table, not wanting to get mired in her trouble, but he had to ask, "What's up?"

"The chicks!" his mother said. "Every . . . single . . . one."

Oh, dear, thought Phillip. Yet it had happened many times before, no matter how tightly they wired the chicken pen. Every year one or two were lost. About one year in three, there was a major slaughter. His mother shouldn't be so upset.

"Coon or weasel?" he asked.

"A weasel wouldn't live here! It was a coon."

"Huh!" He was surprised that even a coon would venture so far into this imitation suburbia. He glanced out the window, seeing for the first time how close the line of trees really was; only four or five streets down, after all.

"Well, never mind," he said. "I'll fix the pen and we'll get some more."

"Oh, Phillip, I don't know, I don't know." She had stopped sobbing, but she gazed down at the tabletop as if in the deepest despair.

What's wrong? Phillip asked mentally, not wanting to ask aloud. Actually, he knew. The chickens were a way of still being country people, even in these surroundings. They were the measure of difference between this yard and every other. They were self-sufficiency, and they were a way of saying that not everything had changed.

He got up and went outdoors, knowing he had nothing to say that could help her. Tomorrow or the next day she would buy more chicks and begin again. Meanwhile he would get things cleaned up.

Thea called him. She was hitched by her leash to the clothes pole. She hated her harness; tried to back out of it or walked around with her body scrunched low to the ground and her head high, making a long, Nefertiti neck. Phillip hated the harness too. It seemed emblematic of everything that was wrong with this place.

He took the harness off and lifted Thea to his shoulders. She wasn't exactly sure she wanted to be there. The purr sounded thin; the four paws teetered, uncommitted.

"All right, you can get down, but stick around, okay?" It was time for Thea to begin stepping out on her own. Ridiculous for them to guard so closely, she who had survived kittenhood on a hog farm.

Yet as she stalked away toward the fence he thought of losing her. How much pain he would feel—they would all feel—if Thea went off exploring and never came back! He thought of his mother crying at the table, and everything that had shaken loose last night in his desperation started to shift again.

"Here, Thea!" He bent and snapped his fingers. Thea felt insecure, so she came to him, rubbing briefly around his legs. She paused, still leaning on him, but looking intently away at a bush. Her yellow eyes glowed.

Abruptly she left him. She ran a little way, crouched, and pounced on a cricket. The cricket squirmed away. She pounced again, all her weight pointed into her front paws. If she came down that way on a mouse or chipmunk, she would probably break its back. The cricket, cushioned somehow in the deep grass, survived, to be sprung after again. Thea's face was full of play.

Phillip didn't rescue the cricket. He restrained himself, too, from capturing Thea and putting her back on the leash. With an effort he turned away and looked into the chicken coop he and his father had built.

He saw the place where they had perhaps used one staple too few. A small hole had been wrenched wider. A few long, soft raccoon hairs fluttered on the wire.

Inside were the silent chicks—some scattered around, half eaten, the rest in a downy yellow heap, streaked thinly with blood. They were too small to make a ghastly sight. They only looked pitiful.

So. Can an animal be evil?

Thea glided past his legs and stepped warily, delicately, across to the heap of dead chicks. She sniffed them, mouth slightly open. With her white, pointed fangs and broad tongue panting back and forth, she looked like a miniature panther. He wondered what she gleaned, all turned inward on her sense of smell. Could she understand, just from smelling, what a raccoon was? Could she understand death?

"Did Thea do that?" asked a voice behind him. The girl!

"No," he said. "Coon."

"Oh!" She looked around at the ranch-style houses; trim, uniform, pastels and reds and blues; at the hedges and fences and mowed lawns and the ornamental cherry trees. "Oh!" she said, in a voice of pleased surprise.

Phillip looked down. "Yeah, well . . . pretty hard on the chicks."

The girl squatted to look in at them. Her face was serious and intent but cool. "A lot of people say that humans are the only animals that massacre like this," she remarked.

Phillip had heard that. "They only kill what they can eat," he said, quoting another bit of folk wisdom.

In the coop, Thea took a chick by the wing and tossed it in the air over her shoulder. She whirled to see it fall, but it landed with a dull, unresilient thump. Too dead to play with. She came out and leapt onto the roof to wash her paws.

"I suppose the coon was just playing too," the girl said. "All those little things moving . . . bite, bite, bite."

Phillip shivered. "That doesn't make any difference to the chick."

"No, but it does to me."

She stood up. Phillip looked at her, trying to decide if she was the same age he was or older. She seemed too confident to be his own age.

"Why does it matter to you?" he asked.

"Because," she said, "I want to know all about animals,

how they're related to people, and what we all want from each other."

"Oh." Older, he thought. He felt discouraged, and his mind wandered to the burial of the chicks. Dig a hole right here in the yard, he supposed. It seemed almost sacrilegious, though. In this whole neighborhood he would be the only person digging a hole in the earth, the only person to despoil the purity of a lawn.

"How come you have chickens, anyway?" the girl asked. "Where do you come from?"

"I come from Illinois. We had a hog farm."

"You had a *farm*? And you came *here*?"

"Yeah. And lemme tell you, in a lotta ways it's a big improvement!"

She didn't seem to expect that, and now she seemed younger, looking around her in puzzlement. Phillip felt glad to be one up on her.

"Farm doesn't mean Currier and Ives!" he said. "It wasn't pretty! It was a great big ugly meat factory, and it stank! If these people living their nice, clean lives in their nice, clean houses could smell it, they'd never eat pork again!"

"You didn't like it at all?"

"It sucked! I hated it. This place sucks too. It just doesn't smell as bad!"

"Anyway," said the girl, "I came for my flashlight. Sorry about the chicks."

Phillip went inside for the flashlight, thinking, Boy, you have just discovered the perfect turnoff! What a genius!

When he came back out, the girl was gone. Thea, too, had disappeared, and when Phillip hurried around the corner of the house, he found them together in the backyard.

Thea was intent in the middle of the lawn; nose a quarter

of an inch from the grass, ears hard forward, tail at alert half-mast. The girl was a few paces behind, bent over in equal concentration.

Thea pounced. Her paws spread wide, like hands, and Phillip briefly saw claws. The flurry was short. Next he saw her tossing something small and gray. As it fell, she scrambled after, and then lay down beside it, as proud and leisured as a Roman on a couch, speaking to the girl. Phillip saw the gray thing move.

"A mole," the girl said, looking up as he came toward them.

Astoundingly the mole was still intact, hurrying away through the grass as fast as it could go. Thea affected not to notice the escape, leaning back luxuriously and speaking to them again. But she watched the mole from the corner of her eye, and when it had gone too far, she pounced and tossed it. The mole squeaked.

Phillip glanced at the girl. Her face was expressionless, but her eyes were bright and interested, strangely like Thea's. She made no move to interfere.

Thea made yet another delighted spring at the mole, and Phillip sprang too. He caught Thea around the middle. She squirted through his hands, but he grabbed again, just in time, and got her by the tail. She squalled, ears flat to her skull, turned, and swatted him. It was no half measure. He heard her claws pop through his skin and saw the blood start. But for the first few seconds it didn't hurt, and he picked her up, though she squirmed and struggled. Her body felt five pounds heavier than normal.

"You're going back inside," he told her, and popped her through the cellar door. He had to slam it quickly. "Sorry," he said, looking in the window. All he could see was a dramatically lashing tail. "Better luck next time."

He wiped the back of his hand down his jeans, smearing the blood. The girl had picked her flashlight up off the grass and was coming toward him, looking annoyed.

"It's perfectly natural for a cat to catch a mole," she said. "She wasn't being cruel, she was only playing."

Thea's angry wail came muffled through the cellar door. Phillip felt surrounded. He looked beyond the girl, seeing a small gray wedge blunder through the grass. He wasn't especially in love with moles, though generally in sympathy with anything that made a life's work of wrecking lawns. He didn't feel suffused with altruistic triumph. Still . . .

"It's perfectly natural for me to save it," he said, and shrugged and turned away.

But he had interested her. She followed him toward the chicken coop, and when he looked, she was frowning at him. "*Is* it?"

"Well, mammals . . ." said Phillip. "Fellow mammals . . ."

"Okay," she said, kindling. "What if you had . . . a gerbil, say, that you liked a lot, and you had Thea, and all of a sudden—let's just say, for the sake of argument—all of a sudden there was nothing left in the whole world to feed her except that gerbil. What would you do?"

What a *ghoul!* thought Phillip; and then, Of course, give the thing to Thea! Then he remembered the gerbil his friend Rob had had in fourth grade, its smooth brown hair and bright black eyes. Oh, damn! Trapped!

He looked up and saw her face, intent as Thea, hunting. Oh no, you don't!

"That will never happen," he said, "so I'm not going to

worry about it. I feed her cat food, and if she catches things, I don't really care, as long as it's not in front of me."

"Inconsistent," she said. Her eyes sparkled.

"Yup," said Phillip. He felt as if he'd like to smile.

"Well, as long as you're aware," she said.

"I'm Phillip," said Phillip. It seemed like time for introductions.

THE BOTTOM LINE

"Listen to this," said Kip from behind the *Rutland Herald*. One hand reached with blind but sure instinct for the coffee cup.

"'Cooper's herd of forty-five milking Saanens'—a Saanen is apparently some kind of goat—'Cooper's herd of forty-five milking Saanens have paid for themselves for the past two years.' *Paid for themselves*, James!"

James rubbed the old toothbrush over the lip strap he was cleaning. The last crust of chewed, dried grass came away, and he looked up. "Pretty good!"

"Whaddaya mean, pretty good? The guy's been at it fifteen years! About time he started breaking even!"

"Well, calm down," said James. The long legs stretching across the space between Kip's chair and the one beside his own had stirred passionately, slopping the grayish water in James's quart yogurt container. He snatched it up as Kip, paying no attention, started to swing his feet down. "Hey, watch it! You almost spilled this!"

A face appeared above the newspaper. Dark eyes flashed scornfully at the yogurt container. "Disgusting! Throw it away and let's go do something!"

"Nothing to do." Kip, his roommate from boarding school, had come to visit and to ski, but it was thirty degrees out and raining steadily.

"No, come on! What do you *do* here all winter?"

James sighed and scraped the toothbrush over the golden bar of glycerin soap. If Kip wasn't here, he might be riding in the indoor ring with Tom and Marion. He might be in Woodstock with Gloria, getting groceries and stopping for a cup of coffee. He might be in his room, studying for his microbiology course. Or he might be writing a poem, trying to get down once and for all his understanding of the art of horsemanship.

"Not much," he said.

Kip swung to his feet and moved restlessly to the window, looking out at gray sky and sodden snow. He made an elegant figure, tall and thin in his jeans and cranberry-striped, button-down shirt. *Très* prep! James glanced down with a slight sense of surprise at his own sweatshirt, moldy-looking from an encounter with the bleach, speckled with grease and suds. His lap was wet where he had laid the straps and rubbed the sponge along them. He smelled of saddle soap.

As if sensing an opening, Kip looked back over his shoulder. "So," he said, "when are you coming back to the real world?"

"I'm not," said James quickly. Then he shook his head, angry with himself for accepting Kip's premise. "Or rather," he said, "I'm in it."

An irrepressible smile broke through Kip's obvious effort to contain it. He primmed his mouth to keep the smile from spreading. "The eighties, James! We live in the eighties. Dropping out is *out!*"

James felt his breath begin to come more quickly. He concentrated on the strap in his hand, rubbing the toothbrush over it until the soap foamed grayish-brown with dirt. "I haven't dropped out."

"Oh, James. James, James, James."

"Look, Kipper, if the place is so far from reality, you didn't have to come!"

"My point, Jimbo! Fine for a weekend—but you're not really going to spend the rest of your *life* here!"

James didn't know, and didn't answer. He dumped the soapy water down the sink, reached under the chair for his soft piece of worn-out undershirt, and opened the bottle of Neat's Foot Oil.

"I think you ought to come back soon, Jimmy, before your brain turns to mush."

"My brain is doing just fine, thank you!"

"James, a guy starts to break even with his goats after fifteen years, and you think that's pretty good! You think you can make money with horses in a backwater place like this, where the only people with bucks are the out-of-staters! Come *on!* If you absolutely have to do this, at least you could go to real horse country. And even then—"

"Kip—"

"Even then the chances are a million to one against you. People don't *make* money with horses, they just spend. Nobody gets rich."

"Kip—"

"And now you're going to tell me you don't want money. Well, to hell with that, James! To hell with it!"

"Kip—"

"Jimmy, I'm gonna call a guy I know at Dartmouth and see if we can find something to do. You want to come along, you're welcome!"

"No," said James. "I'll just sit here and wait for the hospital to call. Better carry our phone number someplace they can find it!"

Half an hour later he stood at the window, watching the friend's Plymouth slither down the long drive. It was a day when none but the foolhardy or the flatlander would venture forth. Gloria was out, but she had the four-wheel-drive. She ought to be back any minute.

The Plymouth disappeared around the corner. James sighed. The house was empty, chill, and damp. He could have gone with them, laughing wildly as they spun over the icy spots, cracking jokes, looking out the window as the white hill country rolled past.

Instead, he hung up the clean, oiled noseband and reached for something else from the pile of leather by the wood box. He came up with a piece of harness.

They were always going to train one of the horses to drive, but it hadn't happened yet. The harness came in every winter to be cleaned, and otherwise hung molding in the tack room.

Could try it on Robbie, thought James. He'd make a cute driving horse. He dreamed ahead to a couple of driving competitions, a couple gold cups. Soon people would be wanting MacLiesh-trained driving horses and would be willing to pay fat sums. . . .

No, they wouldn't. Not enough of them.

Could get a few thoroughbred mares and breed them to Ghazal—start a new strain of warm-bloods. The New England Sport Horse? The Vermont Warm-blood?

Nah.

He glanced at the ticking clock. Gloria should be back now. He wished she were. Gloria was good for taking away thoughts like this. She did her work, and then she sold it. The one activity never seemed to get tangled with the other.

"Damn you, Kipper!" He dropped the piece of harness. Suddenly he was full of schemes, and a dozen sums jostled in his head; addition, multiplication. Yet how ridiculously small the figures were! He remembered Kip last night, talking about his stock portfolio. A sophomore in college, for God's sake!

The strong, assertive engine of the four-wheel-drive pickup sounded in the yard, and a minute later a heavy door slammed. James hurried to the kitchen door and opened it as Gloria skidded onto the step, arms full of grocery bags.

"*Awful* driving!" Her cheeks and eyes were bright, as if she had enjoyed it. "Hey, I thought I saw your friend Kip helping some guy dig out of a snowbank. It was on a really bad hill, so I didn't stop."

"Green Plymouth?"

"Green something." She had the refrigerator door open. "Hand me the milk, James?"

"Yeah, that was Kip."

"Hand me the *milk*, James?" Gloria looked back around

the refrigerator door, and James wiped the smile from his face.

"Sure. Here. Want some water on for tea?"

"Yes. And then I have to go right into the darkroom." She started to unpack the bags.

"Any gossip?"

"Oh! Yeah! There's a for-sale sign on that quarter horse farm."

"*Really?* They've only been there a year and a half!"

"Wicked mortgage, I heard. They thought they'd make enough selling young stock to pay it off, but it costs too much to raise 'em. Plus, nobody around here's into quarter horses."

"Boy, that's too bad!"

Gloria shrugged. "They were doing all right till they decided they had to make a living at it."

"That's right; they used to have that little place on the corner, didn't they?"

"Yes. They sold two or three colts every year and supported their habit. But they're pretty bitter about the whole thing now, or so I hear. They're selling everything."

"Too bad!"

"Well, I don't know." The kettle was whistling, and Gloria poured her tea. "If people get greedy, I don't have much sympathy for them."

She swished the tea bag three or four times through the hot water, plopped it into the wastebasket, and headed for the darkroom.

James slowly mixed himself a cup of instant hot chocolate, reading the list of repellent ingredients on the back of the package as he stirred. Then he wandered to the window, to look out at the dreary yard.

He liked the thought of Kip in his loafers, digging the Plymouth out of a snowbank.

Kip would smile knowingly if he heard about those quarter horse people, and give James that triumphant look. He would think he understood all about it.

But Kip didn't understand, and James thought that Gloria probably didn't, either. Wasn't she herself making every effort to earn a living—if not now, then someday—from doing the thing she loved best? Weren't they all, here at Mac-Liesh Farm? How could you fault someone else for trying? The most you could honestly say was that the attempt had been injudicious.

Musing and looking out at the yard, he saw Tom and Marion leave the barn together. Marion was draped in a long gray-green rain poncho that concealed her almost entirely. All James could see were her hands out in front, waist-high, clenched in light fists with the thumbs uppermost. Clearly they held an imaginary set of reins. By certain indefinable motions within the poncho, James understood her to drive the horse forward onto the bit, while her hands braced delicately against him. She was speaking to Tom all the while, with a shining face that at this distance seemed almost as young as Gloria's.

He didn't have to stay in the house anymore, James realized. With Kip gone, he was free to go to his work again. He set his half-empty mug in the sink and went out to the mudroom to pull on his riding boots.

The rich, pleasant barn smells greeted his nostrils: good hay that they had gotten in this summer by the sweat of their brows; clean horses; pine shavings; and manure. A few heads looked at him over stall doors, with mild interest. He went straight to the white, noble head of his own horse, Ghazal.

"Hi, buddy. Wanna do some work?"

Ghazal would consider it. He dropped his silver moleskin muzzle into James's palm, blowing his breath out gustily.

"Sorry. Treats later." He slipped the black leather halter over Ghazal's bony head, buckled loosely, and led him out to the cross ties in the aisle. Ghazal wore an ugly yellow-plaid blanket, rumpled and stained.

Beneath the blanket he was fairly clean, but James ran a brush over him anyway, for once not tempted to skimp. He spent several minutes on the long silver tail, combing until all the hairs were separate, and swished silkenly. Then he saddled and led Ghazal to the indoor ring.

It was empty and quiet. Ghazal's hoofbeats, even muffled in the sand, were loud. His breath, and James's, puffed white in the dimness. Ghosts shadowed them on every wall; four repeated figures, dark young riders on white horses, moving silently in the mirrors. At every corner James approached himself, then paralleled himself, then left himself behind.

Trot trot, Ghazal—smooth and regular and strong.

He strove to remember, warming up, what it was that he wanted to work on. Transitions, he thought, and did a few; trot to walk, walk to canter, canter to trot to walk . . .

The reins flapped loose. Ghazal wandered at will.

What in hell am I doing this for?

Kip was upwardly mobile. James knew that he himself was likely moving down. He would never again have the degree of affluence he'd enjoyed in his father's house; the certainty of new, expensive cars and far-flung vacations, the easy choice of an expensive restaurant dinner, an expensive education. In the eighties you wanted those things; so they told you.

And who am I to play holier than thou?

Ghazal walked to the door and stopped with his nose to the latch, breathing a sigh. When James did nothing, he nudged the latch suggestively. Here's how you do it, buddy!

"Sorry, fatso. At least you're gonna get some exercise." He turned Ghazal away from the door. Eight or ten laps, and then they'd go back, having accomplished nothing. . . .

No, he knew himself, and as soon as he felt Ghazal's uncommitted, shambling trot, he pushed scoldingly with his legs. No response. He tapped with the whip. A startled surge of power told him he'd gotten through.

This was a good trot, with plenty of impulsion. Impulsion—the energy from the rear that comes forward into a rider's hands and gives him something to work with; like breath support for the singer, turgor pressure for the stalk of celery; like the current that floats the little boat or the wind that fills the sail; like drive and purpose and commitment in the human character. When Ghazal's hindquarters were engaged, so that his hind feet stepped well forward under his body and he carried himself, not pushing himself like a wheelbarrow, and when the fresh energy flowed up his relaxed spine and neck and down onto the bit and submitted gladly to James's hands, then beauty happened, and James was in it. He didn't need the mirrors then.

He could have shouted at the unexpected joy. Instead, he resumed the dull transition work. Ghazal's impulsion changed it to a dance. They danced together.

Then James pushed harder, to find the limits where Ghazal's softness turned to strain. The limits were too narrow still. Gently James nudged against them a couple times, bumped them back maybe a little. Then back to the dance. Then rest—plain old tired walking.

"Good boy! Good boy!" You were supposed to praise your horse after good work. But James felt funny about it. It oversimplified the relationship between horse and rider and work. Ghazal knew his own goodness, and his goodness was his reward. His correct and joyous motion was his pleasure. He only needed James to stimulate him to the effort; then to support him and step out of his way. Ghazal's was the body with the power and the knowledge. Ghazal should be the one to utter condescending praise.

Now the magic moment was past. James dismounted, ran up the stirrups, and began to walk cool his sweaty white horse. Once again they were a couple of ordinary mortals of different species, eyeing one another across a gap of ignorance.

Later, as he buckled on the ugly yellow-plaid blanket, James caught himself dreaming. The dream was a montage of international flags against a blue sky, Olympic TV clips, magazine photos, and Rolex advertisements. Those were for all the parts he knew nothing about.

At the center of the dream, though, was the feeling of the ride just now. He noticed that even in the dream, he shut out everything else to concentrate on that feeling, and to ride as if he were alone.

So I'm already doing my dream, he thought. It's not only for the future. It's now.

He turned Ghazal into his stall and brought him a handful of sweet feed, rich with molasses. He laid his hand on the yellow blanket and felt the warmth of the horse come through. A sudden, clear thought came.

THE SIXTH SENSE

I don't do this for money. I do it because I want to.

It was so simple that he wondered why he hadn't said it to Kip, in so many words. There isn't money in horses, or not much. If it were money he wanted most, he'd be doing something else.

He thought of the guy in the paper, with the herd of milk goats who paid for themselves. The understanding Kip had scattered with his attack returned.

If a guy has been doing all that work for fifteen years before it begins to pay, then he's doing it for its own sake, not for money. Money is great, money is necessary, but it's nothing in itself. It's *for* things—food and shelter and education, and the freedom to do what you want.

And how many of the things people *want* to do ever pay for themselves? Not skiing, certainly. No, you *pay* to ski, and pay plenty. Some people get rich, but not you, Kipper, old man! Put that in your pipe and smoke it!

Kip returned at chore time, flushed in the cheeks and very amusing about the snowbank episode. Time and hot buttered rum had wrought a change of view, James thought. But he was glad to have Kip in better humor.

The evening's chosen amusement for the MacLieshes was a wobbly home video of a three-day event in Pennsylvania. James would have liked to see it, but being a good host he played cribbage with Kip in the kitchen, so the TV couldn't draw his eye.

Even here, though, he could hear the self-conscious voice of the narrator—Tom's ex-student Jennifer—giving the names of horses and riders and points to note. Only once her voice warmed to normalcy, as she gave a rider's name and then exclaimed, *"What a hunko!"* In the living room, Marion and Gloria whistled and clapped; Uncle Tom harrumphed.

Kip smiled slightly and pegged fifteen. "Great entertainment, eh, Jimbo? You're gonna get skunked!"

"Guess so," said James, pegging four. He must see this film later, if only to discover what kind of guy Jennifer would call a hunko.

"Beer?" asked Kip, getting up and going to the refrigerator.

"Okay," said James without thinking. He was looking at Kip, who had taken over the role of host where the beer was concerned with his customary ease. He was measuring himself against Kip and remembering that nothing was certain in this world, wondering if Kip could be wrong about things when he looked so right.

Kip twisted off the caps and flipped them one by one into the wastebasket. He handed a beer to James and roamed a little way across the kitchen, nursing his own bottle against his chest. At last he took a long swig and turned to face James.

"Guess I'll be heading back tomorrow," he said, "if you can drive me to the bus."

"Wait and see what it's like in the morning," James suggested, because he was ashamed of his own relief.

Kip shook his head. As he stood there, reared back a little on his long legs, he looked more serious than James could ever remember.

"Come back with me, Jimbo," he said. "Go to school."

This was not the young male challenge of this morning, the half-laughing struggle for dominance. This was the old good friendship that lay buried so deep beneath the games, they had nearly forgotten it.

123

"I don't want to," said James.

"Why not?"

James opened his mouth to say the things he'd thought that afternoon. They had seemed clear and simple. He had felt sure of them. Now, facing Kip across the kitchen, he realized he was sure of his ideas, but unsure of himself. The truth was there, but would he be true to it? And wasn't it, after all, only part of the truth? There were so many other things in life; things, maybe, that Kip knew about and he did not.

For instance, what if he wanted a place of his own someday? How would he afford it? How would he afford the superb, expensive horses he would someday need to carry him to the top of his chosen profession? Would he ever again hop on a plane for that winter week or two in Bermuda? Money was freedom, he knew, at least in material things. He didn't know how he would react when he came up against the barrier of not having enough.

No, he couldn't open his mouth and preach to Kip about money and satisfactions. Still, something must be said, and the right thing. He could never explain all that was in his heart. He must speak in code and trust Kip to understand.

"Kip . . ." he began helplessly, because the silence had stretched too long. "Kip . . ."

Kip laughed a little, looking down at his beer. "Stubborn old Jimmy," he said. "Well, go for it, then! Go for it!"

His voice was rough and reluctant, his reservations imperfectly concealed. Time, James knew, might dispel the reservations, or it might give them the remembered ring of prophecy. Or things might always be like this; always reservations on both sides and never a clear judgment by fate or fortune.

The Bottom Line

Raucous shouts and whistles broke from the other room. "Oh, my God!" cried Tom in a revolted voice.

Gloria said, "I'm calling her up!" She reached through the doorway and snatched the phone from its table.

Suddenly it seemed imperative to James that he rejoin his family and his real life, and give up being separate here with Kip. He stood up from the table. "I've gotta see this."

Kip slanted an amused glance at the cribbage board, where James's peg lagged far below the skunk point. "Okay, Jimmy," he said, and followed James into the living room to join the others.

THE GREYHOUND

THE FOUR DOGS leapt at the gate, whining and crowding one another. Their beautiful, elongated paws caught at the steel mesh. Bony tails thumped loudly against the fence and each other's haunches. Ears flattened appealingly against long, smooth skulls. Deep eyes glowed with a golden, friendly light.

"They all belong to the same kennel," said Sharon, "or they'd be fighting." She reached through the gate and snapped the leash onto a collar. "Somebody had a rotten weekend at the races."

"They bring them when they don't win?" asked Phillip. He was pushing the other dogs back as Sharon drew her captive through the gate. Freed from the necessity of competing, the greyhound drew itself up in dignified pleasure at being singled out.

"Yes," Sharon said, giving the high neck beside her one reluctant stroke. "I don't know the magic number, but after a while they get rid of the slow ones. It's not like horses, where each one is a huge investment of time and money. There are *so* many dogs. . . ."

"Horses are also good for something besides racing," Phillip suggested, following Sharon and the dog across the parking lot.

"Yes, you can always retrain a racehorse. But these guys—"

"Don't they make good pets?"

"Well, yeah, they do. I've got one. They're *great* dogs—but people don't know about them, or they're not into greyhounds, or . . . I don't know. People are scared they might chase cats because of the way they're trained to run after rabbits. They do have the chasing instinct, though *mine* hasn't . . . but, anyway, there are just so many. You'll see."

Sharon seemed very matter-of-fact about this, and Phillip wondered if he, too, would learn to be.

Growing up on a farm, he'd always known that veterinarians worked as much with death as with life. Unlike doctors, vets were always killing in the course of a day's work. They brought suffering to a peaceful end. They rid the world of surplus pets, and they killed for the convenience of owners who didn't want to be bothered anymore. He'd always known that much of it was dishonorable.

But he didn't think he'd seen or heard of anything more dishonorable than this: the production of hundreds of thousands of beautiful animals for the sole purpose of providing people with something to bet on, and the casual disposal of the ones who proved less fit.

He was supposed to be learning how to do this, so he opened the door for Sharon and watched her lead the reluctant dog into the grooming room, where Dr. Rossi waited with a syringe in her hand.

Sharon made all her movements big and clear so he could understand them. She knelt at the greyhound's side and hugged it around the chest. At the same time she grasped the right foreleg with one hand and pulled it forward. Dr. Rossi approached and took the stiffly offered paw. The dog flattened its ears, still hoping for the best.

Dr. Rossi held the needle pointing straight toward the ceiling a moment as she studied the slender, corded leg. Then she slid the steel point neatly into the bulging vein and depressed the plunger. The dog whined and a second later collapsed.

Dr. Rossi stood up, twisting the disposable needle out of the hypodermic and looking down regretfully at the body. Then she glanced at the needle and tsked to herself. "I keep forgetting, there's no need to preserve sterility." She was a small, fortyish lady with a country-club look; hair just so, face beautifully painted. But her eyes were real, and sad. She turned away to the table for a fresh needle and a refill.

"Pick them up like this," Sharon said in a small voice. She gripped two handfuls of loose skin, at the dog's neck and farther down the spine. The dog hung away from her fists, horribly slack. "And carry them out to the incinerator."

Phillip cleared his throat. "Is it heavy? D'you want help?"

"No, I'll get this one. You can take the next."

The three remaining dogs stood and wagged their tails when the door opened. Sharon carried their companion across the blacktop and left it in the shade next to the incinerator. She unsnapped the leash from the dead dog's collar.

"Okay, next dog!" She was trying to sound cheerful. Phillip wondered why.

Now only three dogs leapt at the fence in happy, jealous expectation. They seemed to have no inkling of what had just occurred, and Phillip was slightly surprised. Many times he'd seen dogs deeply distressed at the death of a friend. Maybe the greyhounds were too excited about going for a walk to pay attention to the smell of death.

Sharon snapped the leash onto the collar of a beautiful fawn greyhound, who bounded joyfully out when Phillip opened the door. Phillip felt helpless and dazed. He looked through the chain-link fence at the two remaining greyhounds, and he wondered what would happen if he let the gate stand open, and walked away. But he didn't do that. He dropped the U-bar with a clank and slowly followed Sharon.

It was too quick and too easy to kill these dogs. He didn't like what that said about life, and he thought of his father, who was shrunken and damaged yet seemed essentially himself. While he seemed himself, they counted on the continuation of things as they had always been. Yet these dogs, so full of life and self one minute, were dead in the next, almost without transition. He thought for a second of calling home.

But that was Not Done; just as it was Not Done to leave the gate open, nor was it Done to fling yourself in Dr. Rossi's way and shout, "Stop!" So he stood again and pretended to study how Sharon held the dog, and then he had to take it by its warm, loose skin and lug it out to the incinerator, its long beautiful legs dangling and bumping against his own. Then he had to take off the leash and go put it on a long beautiful neck like a column, like the neck of a doe, and he had to lead the third dog in to Dr. Rossi's needle.

Dr. Rossi's sad brown eyes found his face and studied him as he stood beside the dog, waiting.

"The needle isn't the worst way to get rid of a dog," she said. He understood her to mean that if they did not do it, someone else would, someone less scrupulous and less efficient. She understood his stubborn, mute look in answer, for she nodded. "Yes, it stinks. But hold the dog, please."

He wrapped the leash around the muzzle as he'd seen Sharon do, not meeting the sad, worried eyes. He knelt and hugged the dog. Its hide was smooth like polished wood. The leg he grasped in his hand was warm, and he felt the pulse jump.

Dr. Rossi approached with the needle, and the dog flinched back.

She stopped and looked straight at him, very serious. "You must hold quite firmly, Phillip. Otherwise the needle will slip out before the full dose is given, and that's horrible."

Phillip, to his surprise, felt tears spill over his lower lids. He gripped the dog's leg more firmly and stretched it forward. Quite close to his face, only slightly blurred, he saw the needle enter the round vein, saw the plunger depress under Dr. Rossi's pretty, lacquered thumb. In a few seconds the dog went limp, like a puppet when the strings are snipped. It seemed to melt out of his arms, sprawling on the floor. Phillip stood up, wiping the palm of his hand across his eyes. Sharon came forward and picked the dog up for him. He followed her out into the sunshine, hearing Dr. Rossi's quiet voice behind him: "Good job, Phillip."

His whole head felt prickly and faraway, as if it floated above his body on a string. He had no thoughts; only followed Sharon on feet that seemed faraway, too, on legs that felt like rubber bands. Through a haze of small black dots he saw the last greyhound on its feet, far to the back of the run.

"I'll get her," he said to Sharon, taking the leash.

He went through the gate, carelessly leaving it ajar. But Sharon was there to push it shut behind him. He walked down the long, long run. The diamonds of chain link blurred past his unfocused eyes.

The greyhound sat as he approached, bony tail clamped between her legs. The golden-brown eyes regarded him gravely for a moment, then shifted away, as if to spare them both embarrassment. She flattened her ears but otherwise ignored him as he snapped on the strong black leash. His hands seemed faraway—everything was faraway.

"Come on," he said, tugging deferentially on the leash.

The greyhound rose to her feet with dignity, still not looking at him, and paced quietly at his right side as he went back down the run. Her head was turned away. She watched the cars on the busy road out front. Her nose twitched as she sniffed the breeze. She did not turn to look at her dead companions, piled near the incinerator. Phillip felt she deliberately did not look at them.

His palms were sweaty on the leash. It could easily slip through his hands. Very slowly, as if at gunpoint, he slid the loop over the wrist for greater security, thinking, It only gets worse. This is the worst yet.

He was careful to address none of his thoughts to the dog. What could he say except, "Sorry, I have to do this"? That seemed craven, because in fact no one held a gun to his head. There was only the force of the people around him, doing a certain distasteful thing in which he had agreed to participate for a fee.

131

THE SIXTH SENSE

They walked across the sunny driveway and came to the door of the grooming room.

Phillip opened it, but the greyhound hesitated, looking at the sky and the trees behind the building. She couldn't really know—she seemed unhappy, but she couldn't know. It was only her beautiful form that gave each movement such significance. He was reluctant to tug on the leash. But Sharon was coming, and so he did. The greyhound turned and came with him into the room.

Dr. Rossi waited with the needle. She looked beautiful, too, in an older-lady way; standing in her long green lab coat under the harsh light. You couldn't blame Dr. Rossi.

Turning his face away, feeling things crack and groan within him, Phillip knelt on the concrete floor. He looped the leash around the greyhound's muzzle and hugged her, reaching for the foreleg. She rolled her eyes at him. Deep within Phillip saw a golden light, grave but friendly. As he embraced her she slowly waved her tail.

"No," he said. He dropped her leg as the steely needle came near.

Dr. Rossi's sad eyes regarded him. "Phillip," she said. "Phillip. We do six dogs a day some weeks. What are you going to do?"

Still hugging the dog, Phillip closed his eyes and let his breath go in an openmouthed sigh. He saw it going on and on. He saw himself carrying dog after dog to the incinerator. He thought perhaps he saw himself getting used to it. What are you going to do?

"I'm going to save this one," he said, thinking, Then, even if I do get used to it, maybe it will be all right.

"Just this one," he said.

The Greyhound

*   *   *

They worked hard to persuade him, Sharon and Dr. Rossi. They said how much exercise a greyhound needed, and that she probably wasn't housebroken. She might chase small animals, they said, and what about that little cat of his?

Thea! In his heart Phillip was cold with terror for her— Thea, his best friend. But it was already too late. He could only go forward and try very hard to make things work.

And no matter how hard Sharon and Dr. Rossi tried, their bright eyes watched him, and they were glad when he didn't yield. Dr. Rossi gave his dog a worm pill and some vitamins. Sharon told him about her own greyhound, and the eleven cats she had saved from the needle in the past three years. He put his dog in the run farthest from the incinerator, out of sight of the dead dogs, and went back to finish his morning's work with a warm, choked feeling inside.

Later it was different. When he took his dog out of the run on a borrowed leash and tried to get her to walk beside his bike, she was plainly frightened. She'd never seen anything like it before. Nor had she seen trucks rushing and rattling past her, garbage cans by mailboxes, houses and horses and garage doors surging open. She did not leap or whine, but she panted, with the corners of her mouth strained back in an ugly grin. Out here in the sunshine, he could see the unhealthy dullness of her hide. Worms, Sharon said. They feed them raw, rotting meat, she said. Phillip, wheeling his bike alongside a dog who whipped around in alarm every time a truck went by, began to feel he'd made a mistake.

He didn't want to admit that. He looked hard at the greyhound and said to himself, "She's alive." So she was not

133

as attractive to him just now; at least she wasn't lying on top of that heap of legs beside the incinerator.

That was undeniable but didn't make him happier. He began to think of shots and dog food, and the necessity to spay her. He thought of school coming up and how he would work after school, and then have homework. That left no time for long runs, and no time to train her; no time to get her used to Thea. Horrible scenes came up in his mind. He crushed them down by thinking what his mother would say, and of his father's distress, that even a dog for his kid was so impossible.

His heart felt heavy, literally heavy, and his shoulders stooped with carrying it. When he looked at the greyhound, he felt only pain. But it was too late now. . . . He could not think clearly, but he knew there was no going back to Dr. Rossi and her needle. The life in this dog meant too much to him, even if the dog herself did not. He'd taken his stand against mortality . . . oh, hell. Oh, hell.

He wheeled his bike past the end of their street and the four streets beyond, heading for the mountain. Where the streets ended, he hid the bike in a bush and began climbing up a barely discernible scratch in the dirt that was the path. The greyhound panted behind him, claws scraping on the rocks. She walked awkwardly on this steep, uneven ground.

They came now to his spot. A piece of the mountain had sheered away here, leaving a bare face of stone twenty feet high, with a heap of shale and rubble at the bottom. It was ringed by trees from which the grapevines hung as big as anacondas. You could swing on them; he hadn't yet, but Kris had, the day she'd brought him here.

That was three weeks ago, and so far as he knew, it was the best place around. Climb any higher and you couldn't help seeing the little pastel houses, all laid out on their half-acre lots. Lower down, you started seeing the cars go by. Here was the only possible place to read Thoreau and think.

Think. He sat on a rock, and the greyhound gingerly stretched herself on the shale beside him. She rested her muzzle on her long graceful paws, but her eyes remained open, following the flight of birds and rolling every once in a while toward Phillip.

He stared at her, but he wasn't thinking of her, nor of the three others who were dead, nor the dozens still to die. He wasn't thinking of his lost home or his sick father. He was thinking of trains: hop on one, ride till it stops; hop off, catch another. He was thinking of country roads: just walk; at every crossroad take the fork that looks best.

He was thinking that he'd never get anywhere. There wasn't anywhere for him. And, anyway, he'd be smashed going through a tunnel, or murdered by a motorcycle gang, hit by a truck. He knew that the worst thing in the world can happen, has happened, will happen. No reason why not. Nothing to stop it.

He was thinking how the needle went into the veins of the dogs' legs, how quickly the dogs collapsed. Looking at the foreleg of the dog he had saved, he saw the very vein Dr. Rossi would have used. He reached out, and the dog raised her head to watch him. He put his fingers on the jumping pulse. He looked at the veins in the back of his hand, big and round, and then he turned the hand over to look at his wrist.

He no longer knew what he was thinking.

Perhaps it was a long time, perhaps a moment, before the dog broke in upon his state by turning her head downhill, pricking up her ears. Phillip closed one hand over the wrist at which he had been staring, and followed the dog's gaze.

135

Kris was coming up through the woods, in jeans and a butter-colored shirt. The sun was bright on her pale hair, and she moved so quietly that he did not yet hear her.

It was extraordinary to see her coming. He could have cried. He wanted to rise up and hug her, press her to his aching chest. But they were not on such terms. He hugged his greyhound instead, for the second time, and laid his cheek for an instant on the smooth dome of her skull.

Kris stepped into the clearing. She stopped and looked at them, saying nothing.

Phillip saw her putting two and two together, knowing that today was his first day of work, perhaps remembering how he saved the mole, maybe knowing something about greyhound racing. She didn't ask questions, just came slowly forward and extended her hand, index finger folded in the shape of a dog's nose for the greyhound to sniff.

The greyhound's long nose twitched. She looked up, and the two regarded one another. They looked alike: tall and strong and racy; hunting creatures.

"Why did your mother ever name you Kris?" he asked, thinking, but people aren't called Artemis anymore!

She looked swiftly at him, starting to smile at the strange question. But the smile slid away.

"My mother doesn't know anything about me!"

Phillip gaped at her. He felt exceptionally strange, as if the world around him had been frozen and was now coming to life. He felt almost seasick, and very small. The three of them were so small under the bare cliff and the thick trees hung with grapevines.

"What's the matter? I thought you two got along OK."

"Oh—get along!" Kris looked off into the trees. "What's

getting along, anyway? It's easy to get along with somebody who doesn't pay any attention."

"I thought your father was the one. . . ."

"Dad at least bothers to fight! Mum just tunes out—it's like I'm not even real to her, like I'm one of her kindergarten kids. My mother turns me into *nothing*!"

Phillip shook his head. Nobody could turn Kris into nothing, though she might feel that way for a time. But it would be sappy to say that. The best thing to do for Kris was to change the subject.

"I saved this greyhound's life," he said, "and now I don't know what to do with her."

The black look fell from Kris's face, and she listened while he told the story, growing full of indignation, and proud of him. "*Good* for you!" she said, and shook his hand. Meanwhile her left hand lay quietly on the greyhound's smooth skull, fitting perfectly.

"I don't think I can keep her," Phillip said. "I'll just take her home awhile and see if I can find somebody to take her. Somebody who doesn't have cats."

"That lets out Aunt Mil," said Kris. She had started to look excited but sobered again, eyes on the greyhound. "I'll ask around—" Her voice suddenly shut off.

Phillip saw her cheeks brighten, and a bold, proud, and challenging sparkle grow in her eyes.

"*I'll* take her."

"I thought your father wouldn't allow pets."

"I don't think," said Kris, feeling her way accurately along the thought, as you feel along a fish bone with your tongue, "I don't *think* he'd actually kill the dog, or take her to the Humane Society. I think he'd rather fight me about it, and I think I can win."

"This leash belongs to the clinic," said Phillip, handing it over.

"I'll get it back to you tomorrow." She was already starting off downhill, impatient for the confrontation. The greyhound rose and followed her, before the slack of the leash was taken up.

Gratitude for you! thought Phillip, watching them go. He was alone again, and he felt cool and light. His heart still ached, but he almost liked the feeling. He was alive and growing.

Far down the hill, beyond the dark lace curtain of tree trunks and big black grapevines, Kris in her yellow shirt turned in a patch of sunshine. She raised one hand in a wave like a salute. The greyhound turned against her leg to look back, too, panting a little.

"Thanks!" Kris shouted to him. "Thanks!"

TANGLE-WOOD

I AM HERE so my father can stay at the hotel and have sex with his girlfriend.

To be just, Nancy is more than a girlfriend. They'll probably marry soon, and then I'll have to admit that I like her quite a lot.

Nancy is extraordinarily beautiful, with long raven hair and sapphire eyes, the sort of cheekbones you see only on TV, and the tall leggy figure of a healthy model. And she's nice, which complicates things. I like to think of her as a soap-opera homewrecker, cruel and calculating. Or I like to think, Anyone that beautiful *has* to be brainless!

Not true. Nancy sometimes says, "I know this is difficult

for you, Marcy." But if I act like a shit to her, she doesn't take it lying down. She gets mad; she says things she's sorry for later, as anyone would. She makes it clear that this isn't the easiest situation for her, either.

Nancy knows how to tell a story so people listen, and she never forgets the punch line. She cooks wonderfully, but she's not above take-out Chinese. She's a talented potter who has made a living at it. She loves animals, she loves gardening, she loves my father. Altogether pretty hard to hate, though I'm trying.

Actually she's like my mother, which makes sense. I don't see how he could help being knocked over by her beauty; and, getting to know her, it seems inevitable that he'd fall in love. He loves my mother, too, because of course she didn't stop being beautiful, talented, and funny when Nancy appeared. She isn't worn-out. If it would only work, I'm sure my father would prefer to have them both. I feel sorry for my father. I think he's very innocent.

My mother was innocent, too; pursuing her career—Paris one week, Mexico City the next—assuming matters at home would stand still until she had time to deal with them. They did, for a while. But my father, bored and lonely, went to that one party too many, and there was Nancy. So he innocently fell in love and told my mother, hoping for God knows what. Their divorce has been official for six months. They are still snarled together like a tangle of barbed wire.

I was also innocent. They just happened to be my parents. It could have been anyone else, and I wish it was.

Here I am, then, in the cellar-bedroom of a suburban sort of house in the Berkshire hills of Massachusetts. We're here for a week of Tanglewood, the summer music festival. There was only one room available in my father's favorite hotel, so we were all going to sleep there, until I found the ad for this place. I said I wouldn't mind staying by myself, and I don't. I'm independent, like my mother, and I prefer to feel I'm not in anyone's way.

When we arrived, it was already dark. My eyes were dim from tiredness and staring at headlights. My father nosed the car into the driveway, still unsure even though the directions had all proved accurate. The yard light was on, and we could see the glow of a television in the living room. It was a mixed signal. Someone was expected, maybe us, but nobody hovered at the window waiting.

We all got out, stretched, and together started up the walk to the front door, my father in the lead. Man, woman, and child—what a nice little family!

But I was glad to have my father there taking charge, and even glad of Nancy's presence. Her accepting silence seemed to assure me I'd be welcome in their hotel room, should this place prove unsuitable.

We went up the cement walk between the stiff rows of yellow marigolds and red-hot salvia, ghastly in the yard light. My father knocked on a door that had three small windows descending across it like stairs. I waited behind him for a surprised face to appear.

But no, this woman had been expecting us, and was even relieved. She was a stocky middle-aged woman; pleasant-looking in a plain way. She wore blue jeans and a flannel shirt. Her hair was cut in a silver bowl around her head. She had big teeth.

"Hello," she said. "You would be the Martins?"

"Uh—yes," said my father, in some confusion. "Uh—this is Marcy, who'll be staying."

"Hello," the woman said again. She advanced a hand for

me to shake. "Vivian Bradley." Her palm was pliable, pink, and firm. Vivian.

She led us through the living room, where another woman of remarkably similar aspect sat watching TV, and downstairs to the cellar. She explained again, as she had over the phone, that this was once a small apartment where the former owner's son had lived. Just a bedroom, kitchen, and bath . . .

The kitchen, through which we were passing, was clean and bare, with a strange wooden platform in the middle of the floor. On the counter were half a dozen small, stainless-steel pails with hoods, all clean and gleaming; bottles; a collander; and a small wooden rack set in the sink with white cheesecloth draped over it.

"Oh, one thing I should have mentioned," said Vivian, preparing to open the bedroom door. "I bring the goats in here, six in the morning and six at night. I'll try not to disturb you."

"*Goats!*" Nancy was incredulous, then delighted. "Of course, that's a milking stand, isn't it?"

Vivian was surprised. "Yes, it is." She was reassessing Nancy and willing to explain. "We never use this kitchen, and it just occurred to me how convenient and sanitary it would be."

"And warm!"

"Oh, yes. It's quite pleasant." Vivian opened the bedroom door. "So . . . if you're awake, Marcy, you can have a glass of fresh goat's milk. Or I'll bring down a cup of coffee and milk a few squirts into it; like cappuccino."

"Oh, *wonderful!*" breathed Nancy. I could see her half wishing *they* could stay here, instead of me.

The bedroom was square, and nothing could conceal its

cinder-block character. It was obviously a spare storeroom, with boxes piled in one corner, fishing poles, canes, and crutches leaning in another. Vivian showed me the half-full closet, where I could put my clothes, and how to work the shower, which would scald you if you didn't know the trick. The phone was in the kitchen/milking parlor.

My father brought in the suitcase and made sure I would be given breakfast, as well as goat-milk cappuccino. He gave me their number at the hotel, and he brought me close and kissed my forehead.

"All right, Marcy?"

"Yup."

"You know where to call me."

"Yeah."

"Well, we'll see you around nine, then. Okay?"

"Okay."

They left. I watched them up the stairs; my father thin and elegant, with a weird face like a battered alley cat's; harsh, pitted skin and clear green eyes full of light. Nancy, tall, strong, raven-haired, beautiful, talking excitedly about the goats until the door at the top of the stairs cut off her voice.

Vivian offered me milk and cookies. I said no. Then she said not to hesitate if I needed anything but to come right up—thinking it odd, doubtless, that I should be abandoned here by my parents—and then she said good night.

I've decided I'm not that thrilled about a parade of goats past my door at six in the morning. If Nancy thinks it's so great, *she* should have stayed. I'm not thrilled with the cinder-block bedroom, or the stiff yellow marigolds lining the walk, or with Vivian. I'm going to brush my teeth, put on a nightgown, and call my mother collect. I hope she won't say anything derogatory or untrue about Nancy, because I don't feel up to being just.

I went to bed in expectation of a disagreeable awakening, but this morning, due to the mysterious alchemy of sleep, I am a different person; a softer person, a person who has forgotten many complications. Under one blanket, lying on a pillow in the dim light, I hear muffled sounds beyond the door, footsteps and a friendly conversational voice. I don't think the sounds awoke me. I'm just awake because I expected to be.

A bare, square little room where nothing is mine, save the contents of one brown suitcase. Weak sunlight comes through the single rectangular window, high in the wall. The sounds, outdoors as well as in the kitchen, emphasize the quiet here. I narrowly miss thinking of my phone call.

A clatter—hooves on linoleum. Suddenly the kitchen sounds empty. Voices in the yard . . . voices? I think some are animals.

I stand on the bed to look out the window, but it faces the wrong way, toward the front walk, marigolds and salvia. The bathroom!

There is no bathroom window.

I'm walking slowly back to bed when I hear a scrabble, rush, and lunge, and a hushed voice cries, "Leah! *Shhh!*"

Last night I was a blasé teenage shit, and by afternoon I'm sure I'll be one again. But right now I'm putting on a bathrobe and going out to see this goat.

She is piebald, big-bellied, hairy. Her udder is enormous: two huge, fat cones hanging close to the ground. She's on the milking stand with her head between the front bars, eating grain; her tongue chases the kernels with an incredibly fast lipping sound. Like a lady lifting skirts out of the mud, she elevates her long flared ears.

Seeing me in my doorway, her yellow eyes shift, and she utters a muffled sound with her mouth full. Vivian, who sits on a three-legged stool and milks hard white jets into a stainless-steel pail, turns her head.

"Oh. Good morning."

"Good morning." I like the sound the milk makes going into the pail, the hard hiss and foam. I come out farther. The linoleum is clean and cool to my bare feet, but from door to milking stand lies a trail of hay and goat-buttons. There is a sharp smell of disinfectant in the air.

"This is Leah," says Vivian.

"Hi, Leah."

Leah has finished the grain, and given up hope of finding stray oats in the corners of the box. She lifts her head to look at me. Her yellow eyes are clear, with rectangular pupils. She appears to think about me. I go closer.

"May I pat her?"

"Yes," says Vivian.

I put out my hand, thinking to pat Leah's neck. But she intercepts the hand and sniffs it thoroughly. It seems only courteous to wait till she is satisfied. I notice that her eyes roll slightly upward, as if in pious contemplation of heaven.

At last Leah looks away, allowing my hand past to touch her neck. Her hair is coarse. Her neck is lean and stringy.

The jets of milk come thinner and weaker, until there is nothing. Vivian stands with a grunt and a puff, then takes the pail to the counter. There she pours the milk through a cheesecloth, which is stretched across the top of a pail. She takes off the cloth, drops it into a pan of sudsy water in the sink, and, using a funnel, pours the milk into quart juice bottles. Immediately it goes into the refrigerator, which holds only milk and short brown bottles of injectable medicines. She squirts red-brown iodine into both pails and swirls steaming tap water through them. She takes a fresh cheese-cloth and pins it across the top of the straining pail.

"Would you like coffee now?" she asks.

"Yes."

She calls up the stairs. "Pat? We'd take some coffee! And Marcy's up, so I guess you could start breakfast."

"Be right back," she says to me. She picks up a coffee can from the floor, releases Leah, and is towed out the door. I would like to follow, but I wasn't asked, and I want to keep my bare feet on the clean section of linoleum.

Vivian and Leah disappear. There is quiet, then a confused trampling sound. I hear Vivian expostulating, and after a moment she reappears, towed by another goat. Her feet barely seem to touch the earth between enormous strides. The goat's eyes bulge. Her tongue flips audibly over her lips; *thup thup thup!* She and Vivian careen through the door, and the goat leaps onto the stand. Vivian dumps the measure of grain rattling into the box and closes the bar on the goat's neck. She collapses onto her stool with a loud puff.

"Phew! This is Amy."

"Hi, Amy," I say, and pat her neck. She rolls a bright eye my way but doesn't stop gobbling for a second.

Vivian wrings out a yellow throwaway cloth into a little plastic bucket of disinfectant solution and carefully wipes Amy's huge udder. Then she dries it, reaches for her stainless-steel pail, and begins to milk. Amy pays no attention. I think, watching, how this animal is distorted—all udder. A mouth, a digestive system, exist only to produce milk.

But if Amy, and Leah before her, are milk factories, they

still seem quite different from dairy cows I've met. If their udders are man's, their minds are reserved for themselves.

I hear steps on the stairs and smell coffee. Pat comes in, carrying three white diner mugs on a metal tray. She nods to me, smiling with her bright, frosty-blue eyes. We decide to go on as if we have been introduced.

She gives the mugs to Vivian, one at a time. I'm uneasy when the steaming mugs pass beneath Amy's hairy belly but don't see anything fall in. Vivian shoots a jet of milk into each and the surface foams, turning pale. She passes the first cup to me.

The coffee is still nearly too hot, but it's good—not that I know that much about cappuccino. I see Vivian hurry to finish Amy as the white mug steams beside her on the counter. When she is done, Pat strains the milk while Vivian takes up her mug in reverent haste. She sits peacefully on her stool, leaning against the cabinets. Sun comes in. Milk trickles through the cheesecloth into a pail, a tiny sound like a running brook. Amy's stomach gurgles.

She has long since finished her grain but doesn't appear to mind waiting. Every thirty seconds she checks the box again, tinkling her bell—just in case. Otherwise she looks at us, occasionally uttering a whispered comment: *"Meh! Meh!"*

"Two left," Vivian says at last, nearing the bottom of her mug. "How's breakfast?"

"Coming."

"How many goats do you have?" I ask.

"Seven," says Vivian. "Plus the babies."

"Wow!"

"Come out and see them," Vivian says, draining her mug and getting up. I get my sneakers and follow.

Amy's udder is thin and floppy now. She rushes along with

147

Vivian attached to her collar, then stops suddenly, wrenching Vivian off-balance as she dives her nose into the lawn. I see why. There's practically no grass left in the goat pens. They look brown and bare.

The goat pen isn't like the blue suburban house. There is a barn in three distinct segments, made of three different materials: asphalt shingles, plywood, and old barn boards. The segments escalate in size and squareness.

There are two fenced areas, one nearly featureless. The other contains two old apple trees, a couple of weathered, flat-roofed doghouses, and several of those giant spools that telephone wire comes on. Four piebald goats with flabby, milked-out udders are standing on them in experimental attitudes.

Amy is ushered through the gate to join them. Vivian goes into the shed with her grain can, and I go to the gate of the other pen. There, the last two goats are crowding. I want to meet a goat that's a free agent, before she gets her nose into the grain.

These goats' minds are halfway to the grain. Their golden eyes have followed Vivian to the shed. Their hooves rattle and scramble on the gate, which is a pallet on hinges. They pay little attention to my hand as I try to pat them.

I feel rude. I'm trying to dab little strokes on their Roman noses, without even asking. I stop.

They appreciate that. The dark gray goat pushes her nose up into my face. It is a bold, surprisingly intimate move. I am shocked and stand still. Her nose is less than an inch from mine. I am tickled by sweet hay-breath and fine whiskers. She puffs gently on my face for several seconds, thinking.

But now the grain rattles in Vivian's coffee can, and the

goats' attention is claimed. They jostle for position; their hooves slip and scramble on the pallet.

Vivian opens the latch, and my goat is the one who slips through. Vivian follows her. She is trotting toward the cellar door, snatching mouthfuls of grass along the way. The remaining goat ignores me. She runs in circles with head high, long ears flying. She bleats in staccato bursts, like machine-gun fire. Hysterical.

In the other pen, the goats lie or stand on the spools and houses. They watch their hysterical comrade, and they watch the cellar door. Their golden eyes are calm, enigmatic. Occasionally they murmur a comment: *"Meh!"*

How haughty they look, the Roman-nosed goats, with their amber eyes and their beards wagging! They are not beautiful, as I'm used to judging it; not like cats. Yet like cats, they give an impression of sage maturity—not the hysterical one but the others, yes. Like a congregation of grandmothers in some old ethnic neighborhood, so knowing of each other's ways that no words are needed.

I want to go in and learn the name of the goat who sniffed my face. I hope she'll do it again.

Her name is Tony. She's seven. She has twins every year and gives a gallon of milk at the peak of her lactation.

That's not what I want to know.

I want to know why, as her sweet breath bathes my face, my heart is stilled in peace.

I follow outside again and watch as she is turned in with the others. She goes to sniff another goat—I can't remember who it is—then hops on the empty stool, turns broadside to the sun, and lies down. She looks at me with her golden eyes as she begins to chew her cud.

THE SIXTH SENSE

I'm still there when Vivian returns with the last goat. When she's put it with the others, she goes somewhere in the barn and opens a door. A stream of baby kids pours out into the empty pen.

The kids are silky, shiny, smooth. Their long ears are soft like rabbits' ears. They bounce and gambol, square off at each other in wicked duels. They are wonderful. Vivian is proud, and I know she expects ecstasy from me. But after I've watched awhile, I feel uneasy and am drawn back to the older goats. They seem more important.

Vivian stops beside me and spends a few minutes telling me how they're all related, who is grandmother, who sister and cousin. I don't care. I look at them. One goat, to whom I was not introduced, gets slowly to her feet, steps down from the roof of her doghouse, and comes to the fence, where she presses her head against Vivian's palm.

"Breakfast!" Pat calls through the window, and we go inside. There's sausage, melon, biscuits, juice, and more coffee. They have a *Boston Globe*, and we divide the sections. We don't mean to get to know each other; just have breakfast comfortably.

I'm brushing my hair when I hear the car. The wide-open ease of my heart begins to tighten a little. I go outside.

Nancy's already with the goats. They are less lazy than an hour ago, and several crowd at the fence making Nancy's acquaintance. She's laughing as their breath tickles her face. Behind her, my father beams his cat smile at the picture she makes. Already the two of them seem happier. I think briefly of my phone call, but it isn't time yet.

"Marcy!" My father's smile is for me now.

Nancy turns from the goats and arches her perfect brows. "You look rested," she says.

Vivian is coming out. She stops halfway down the marigold walk and calls, "Would you like coffee?"

Nancy looks at my father, and he looks at his watch. "Yes, we have time," he says. "Just milk, no sugar."

Pat and Vivian both come. Everyone stands near the goat pens, talking. Vivian likes Nancy. People do, once they've overcome the initial hostility. Anyone as beautiful as Nancy automatically raises hackles at first. It's a great tribute to her character that she has so many friends.

They watch the kids play and talk about goats.

"They're the *brightest* animals," says Vivian. "And so restful."

"Restful?" Nancy asks, watching the kids rear high and crash their heads together. I am listening hard, because I think I know what Vivian's talking about.

It seems so incongruous. Goats are capricious, and eat everything. Yet Pat and Vivian are restful people. They have a stillness at the center, which relates to this penful of goats.

Sadly Vivian is as much at a loss as I. "The Old Ladies," she says, looking at them on their spools. "I don't know," she says. "But I'm a coffee-and-cigarette person, I really am, and I can be a stinker. But the girls make me as peaceful as . . . I don't know. Maybe it's just me."

No, I think. No.

"I've always heard," says Nancy, curling her long beautiful potter's fingers around her mug, "that a goat will calm a nervous racehorse. Some kind of chemistry . . ." Vivian's face lights up with pleasure and comprehension. "I never understood that, either," says Nancy, and they both laugh.

151

But now it's time to say goodbye, and we are off to Tanglewood, where music and a picnic will be our delights. I'm in my usual backseat spot, with nothing to do but look out the window and think.

Last night when I called my mother, she seemed both nervous and elated. I didn't immediately know why. She asked about where I was staying and groaned with me about the six A.M. goat parade.

Then she asked about our seats for this evening's concert. Were they good seats? In the middle? Did I know the numbers?

No, I didn't. I'd probably never seen the tickets, and my mother should know that. She used to be the one in Nancy's place, on our Tanglewood week. She knows how it works.

We are here; parking, walking over the green, dewy grass. My father sees someone that he meets here every year. He stops and introduces Nancy. His rough skin reddens all the way to the tips of his ears. Two years since my mother last came with us. One year she was in Lima. The next was the beginning of Nancy.

Her short hair would be as bright as poppies in this sun. She'd stir restlessly, like a thoroughbred at the gate, swinging the picnic basket in her hand. She'd say decisively, "Well, come with us, then!" Or she'd look off across this lawn and wave to someone else. When she arrives at this evening's concert, there will be many to know her and my father, many to wonder.

While they talk, I drift away to the tent from which Robert J. Lurtsema is broadcasting his radio show. He's rhapsodizing over the Berkshire hills. I watch keenly. No, he does not now put on the wrong record, but he doesn't quite catch the first note, so he lifts the needle and starts again. This gives me a homey feeling, a small comfort.

As it happens, my mother and Nancy have never set eyes on each other.

"I don't see why I shouldn't," my mother said last night. "Tom asked me—I haven't been to Tanglewood in two years, and I'm flying out to Milan the next day, so . . . do you think you're sitting in the middle somewhere?"

I think I'll have a terrible headache tonight. I feel it coming on.

Later we picnic. Nancy has brought good wine, Brie, chewy French bread, lots of fruit. Friends of my father's join us—annual friends, whom Nancy has never met. She is quiet. Her face looks smoothly serene, a glaze. I suspect she's working hard not to seem shamefaced, and I respect her. In a similar situation I imagine I would gabble.

How will she hold up when she comes face-to-face with my mother?

My mother will wear one of her radiant silk dresses, and pearls. She'll be all hotted up with nervous excitement, vibrant enough to make even Nancy feel plain. She'll overrun them both with a rush of talk in her light, carrying voice. My father will long for her. He'll ache for Nancy—the Other Woman, identified before a throng of acquaintances. His face will redden, and he'll be unable to speak. Tanglewood will hurt him like a burn, long after.

Seeing Nancy, my mother will also feel plain, lightweight, and frenetic. She'll want to cry.

I see a kid that I usually meet here. To avoid him, I drift a little apart from my father and Nancy. My father's so distinctive, he'd be like a lightning rod for anyone trying to spot me.

Why shouldn't Nancy have this shock? Look at the shock she's given us.

Why shouldn't my father be humiliated? He's been unfaithful, careless.

Why shouldn't my mother, for that matter, get a shock? She was arrogant. She assumed too much.

Someone taped the morning concert, and we are hearing it again—the beautiful, silvery music of Mozart, sprightly, orderly music you could almost dance to. I stretch out on the grass and bury my face in my arms. If only things were like that!

I think it's unfair for a kid to have to face all these complications growing up. Growing up is hard enough already.

I think it's unfair when people shelter me, act like I can't, or shouldn't, understand these things. I'm not a fool.

The thing I hate most is not being able to think a thought straight through and stick to it.

I hate Nancy! That doesn't work for two minutes.

It's unfair for things to be so complicated! But I know—I know it's not just *my* life here.

They were all fools. Or maybe they were just too innocent for this world.

I am wounded. I am made strong. I can't recall one thing without bringing to mind its opposite, and everything in between.

It makes me quiet, and since my face is downcast, I probably seem sullen. We're having dinner, in our favorite Tanglewood restaurant. I'm having my favorite food, their incredible beef burgundy, and to my astonishment, it tastes as wonderful as it always has. I spoon it in ravenously, trying to fatten up on this joy.

I see my father worrying about me, feeling guilty.

Soon Nancy does too. I should flash them a brilliant smile and start chattering, but I only slurp up the beef burgundy and think my convoluted thoughts. They discuss, when they discuss anything, the evening's program.

I do have a minor headache, a combination of too much sun and too much thinking. I could build on it and spend the evening at Vivian's. But then I won't know what happens.

We finish and drive back to Vivian's so I can change. It's still quite light out. Past six, though; the goats will have already been milked.

They're all in the pen by the barn, where they spend the night. Two particularly piebald creatures press heads together, near the gate. It looks more comfortable than aggressive. I see Tony in one of the barn's three doorways, chewing her cud.

"Is there time for me to see the goats a minute?"

My father checks his watch. "A little time."

Vivian has come halfway down the walk. "May I go in with the goats?" I call.

"Yes. Just close the gate carefully."

She keeps coming down the walk, and my father goes politely to talk with her. Nancy hesitates. I am going to the goats.

They look up calmly, alertly, as I approach the gate. My hand rattles the latch. Long ears lift. They begin to step toward me; I slip through and hastily close the gate. Ears drop. They stop and wait. I go straight to Tony.

She swallows her cud and lifts her Roman nose to my

155

face—puff, puff, puff. Mildly her golden eyes gaze heaven-ward.

She looks down and across the goat yard, where her piebald relatives are pressing heads again. She burps up an-other cud and chews, a steady, rhythmic grinding. She presses her neck against my thigh. Tony.

Shadow. Nancy. She's come through the gate and stands before us, looking at Tony. She gives a little sigh. For the moment her serenity goes deeper than a glaze. Like me, her heart is stilled.

"My mother is coming tonight," I tell her.

She looks up with calm, clear eyes, like Tony's. She sees more, of course. I don't know what Tony sees looking at me, but I think Nancy sees this whole day.

"Are you afraid?" I can ask her anything with Tony here.

Nancy shakes her head, a beautiful calm, sure motion. She stretches one of her long, strong potter's hands to Tony, who swallows her cud and sniffs politely. Then she withdraws her big Roman nose and presses deeper against my leg.

"I appreciate your telling me," says Nancy. "It's nicer not to be surprised. But . . ." Her eyes sharpen on my face. She wonders whether, standing here by quiet Tony, I want to talk. I do. I do. I do.

"Your parents are fine people," Nancy says. "Your father has said *nothing* but good to me about your mother. But . . . about their marriage, they weren't very smart. I myself am not blameless . . ." Her lovely cheeks redden as she says this. I see a wounded look in her eyes.

"But," she says, "whether this pleases you or not, I assure you that I will not make the same mistakes your mother and father did. It's not that I'm a better person, but I know how to make things."

Tanglewood

I don't understand.

"When you are making something," says Nancy, "you give your attention just as long as it's required. There is never a moment when you can look away, until it's done. A human relationship is never done."

I want to reply, so this will be a conversation, but the most I can manage is a nod. But I meet Nancy's sapphire gaze and let her know I understand. Into the Tony-stillness of my heart comes a deeper stillness, of human certainty. Nancy. Nancy.

"Girls!" my father calls. "I think we'd better get moving."

I break free of Nancy's gaze to look down at Tony, dark gray goat. She lifts her nose to me again, puffs her sweet breath on my face. Tony, Tony, what have you done for me?

She lets me hug her. She stands, quiet and accepting. With my ear pressed against her barrel, I hear tremendous digestive processes going on.

Now I run to the cellar bedroom, to yank my dress off the hanger and pull it on.

The auditorium is filled with well-dressed people and a hum of chatter. People stand, knowing they'll have to sit a long time. They scan the crowd for acquaintances, clustering in knots and skeins.

Nancy has told my father. He stands with hands in pockets, subdued. Nancy carries on the conversations with people who have come up to us. I crane my neck, looking all around. I check out all the bright dresses.

She's closer than I think, though. When I see her, she's almost here. She wears a yellow silk dress. Beside her is a handsome man in a dark suit. He looks like an advertisement or a doll. He's no one she's serious about; I see that at a glance.

She's searching, pretending not to, chattering, but all the while her eyes hunt through the suits and dresses. It's hard for me to believe she can't spot my father instantly.

I see the moment when the yellow dress stops moving, when my mother's eyes fix on us. She stands very still, looking. The man doesn't see.

Now, slowly, almost stiffly, she comes toward us. She moves through the people without seeing them, never seeming to touch, not noticing when someone addresses her. The man loses her, finds her again, follows.

At last she stands before us. My father has seen her now, and so has Nancy. The man they were talking to melts away. The chatter of people around us seems to recede, as if we are standing within a bubble. The handsome man is left outside.

We all look at one another.

We are helpless in our looking. We are all trapped in pain, caught by old mistakes that can't be undone. We thought we had something to say, but now we see the hopelessness. Words are only words.

I'm wondering how it can be so, because we're all smart people, cultured and unaccustomed to traps. And this is a strange trap, made of love; almost a beautiful trap.

Nancy. In Nancy's face I see again serenity. Not a glaze; it goes straight through. She doesn't pretend that none of this hurts, but she accepts the hurt with a creaturely calm that makes me think of Tony. More complex; I see that she is sympathetic to my mother, curious, respectful, wary. But, like Tony, she's just looking, just being.

My mother sighs, stirring the front of the yellow silk dress. Her shoulders drop from their high, tense position. Her eyes become softer, tired. All right, I hear her saying as she does at last when the stubborn world has refused to rearrange itself for her. All right.

I look at my father, watching us all. I think there are tears in his eyes. But he is also smiling, as if impossible love and joy are hurting in his chest.

I'm beginning to hear the people again, and behind them, the almost-music of the orchestra tuning up, getting ready to play something good.

WINNING

I was halfway down the hill before I remembered that Dad wasn't even home now. He was golfing and wouldn't be back till supper. I stopped at the end of the path, trying to decide.

Mum was home, and I could go tackle her. It would be like dynamiting a cream puff; but it might be wisest to have her neutralized before the big blowup with Dad.

But from here, taking the back way and cutting across the athletic field, it was a mere twenty-minute walk to Aunt Mil's. I didn't need my courage fired up; I needed my brain cooled and sharpened. I should go to Aunt Mil's.

Only in crossing the athletic field did I truly begin to see and think about the dog. Normally I don't like to walk. It seems slow and laborious, compared to riding a bike. But now I had so much nervous energy that walking was effortless. My head felt a mile above my feet, and my hair flapped out with every stride, the little ends quivering in the breeze. The dog kept pace, in a marvelously slow, springy trot, so arrestingly beautiful that I was forced to drop my own concerns and look at her.

She ought to be nervous, I thought. That was the stereotype for racing animals. This dog was . . . well, perhaps she was nervous. I could see it in her expression and the way she held her tail. But she was self-contained and dignified, like the kind of person who gets ulcers but never uses the wrong fork at dinner.

I clucked my tongue at her. She looked up and I saw deep in her eyes a grave smile. Her tail waved once.

A smile? Ridiculous! Worse—anthropomorphic! If an animal seems to smile, it is only because the human observer is fooling herself, or doesn't know what else to call it.

On the other hand, what is a smile, and what is laughter? The people who study these things give no clear answer. Smiling is said to be related to fear and appeasement, a conclusion based on studies of the grimaces and hoots of the great apes when threatened.

Others claim laughter as one of the great distinctions between man and animal.

To me it's obvious that these are but two strands of the truth, frayed and broken by our culture's sharp-edged definitions. Someday I'd like to be the person who twists the two ends back together.

Boys were playing at the farthest end of the field, kicking a soccer ball around. I'd have to walk by them to get through the fence, which ends there against the oak-covered knoll. I'm not afraid of boys. Most of them are stupid, and living with Greg has taught me how to punch. But touching the high neck of the greyhound, on a level with my hip, I understood why fearful people keep dogs.

One of the boys was Greg—the most graceful and elegant dribbler, the one with the precise, powerful kick. Soccer is what Greg is best at, and he deserves a better team than ours. Even on a really good team, he might be a star. I don't like him, but I stopped to watch as he feinted and dodged through three opposing players, controlling the ball perfectly, right up to the minute when he drove it slanting through the goalposts.

Someone said bad-natured things to him in a good-natured voice, and then I heard the word *sister*. Greg turned to look.

A second later he was striding across the grass toward me, and his face looked exactly like Dad's. "Kris!" he thundered, "what the hell—" His voice sliced off abruptly. He stared, goggle-eyed, at the greyhound.

I glanced down and saw that she was staring back at him. She was perfectly quiet, perfectly polite, only her upper lip curled back to show a set of nice white teeth.

"This is my new dog, Greg," I said.

Greg gave me a look of complete dislike and turned away. "Okay," he called. "Who's having spaghetti for supper tonight? That's the house I'm goin' to."

I smoothed my hand down the dog's beautiful neck, and we slipped away through the oak trees.

Aunt Mil was in the garden under a shady straw hat, picking cherry tomatoes into the basket on her arm. From a distance she looked straight and light, as a daughter, had she had one, might look today. It was only as she approached the fence that the creased, tired skin showed.

"What's this?" she asked and, standing there on the opposite side of the fence, listened to the greyhound's story. The dog meanwhile pressed close to my leg, giving Aunt Mil an occasional reserved glance. Aunt Mil appeared to share the reserve. When I had finished, she only stood there with her lips folded, as if she wanted to consider carefully before she spoke her mind.

"I'll bring tea and gingersnaps out to the picnic table," she finally said.

I led my dog out back and tied her to the table leg. She only stood there, waiting. So many things had happened to her today, one after another. She must be expecting some new change at any moment.

"Come here," I said, sitting on the end of the bench and holding out my hand. She pushed her nose under it once, but then stood looking away as I stroked her. I thought the situation might be easier if she were a more demonstrative animal, if she showed the stress of this extraordinary day with a whine or a shiver. Then I could lose myself in sympathy and maybe even work my father up to a sense of pity. The coming fight was uppermost in my mind, but for a second I wondered if I really was going to like this dog.

Aunt Mil came out with the tray. She set it down and, still standing, poured herself a tall glassful of iced tea. She took four thirsty gulps and stood studying the dog.

"One doesn't think of them as being so muscular," she said. Instantly I noticed, for the first time, the smooth roundness of her haunches.

"She's very beautiful," said Aunt Mil. She drained her glass and set it down. "I'm proud of Phillip. Sometimes I

163

think his troubles have nearly crushed him, but . . . when you push him, you find that his back is already against the wall, and he won't go any farther. I think he'll be all right."

I remembered how weird Phillip seemed, up by the cliff, but didn't say anything. Anyway, he was a lot better by the time I left.

"But you, Kris," said Aunt Mil. "I'm afraid you may have gone too far."

That was exactly what I feared, which left me not much to say.

"Well," I said finally, "it's not as if he has any good reason for not having animals."

"He has all the reason he needs," said Aunt Mil. "He doesn't like them, and it's his house."

"It's my house too!"

Aunt Mil only smiled at me with narrowed eyes.

"Well, it is! At least—it's *Mum's* house!"

Her expression didn't change.

"It's *going* to be my house, or I won't stay!"

"Is that the truth, Kris, or bravado?"

I shrugged. "I don't know. The truth, I guess."

"You have a place here, of course, though I'd prefer not to risk my cats."

"I wonder how she'll be with them? Where's Pish?" Pish was the new tricolored kitten.

"In the living room," said Aunt Mil. "She broke my oldest vase and spilled the Canterbury Bells all over the carpet. Yes, why don't you see if the dog will eat her?"

I was glad to walk away from the two of them, old lady and solemn dog, and step into the cool, quiet house.

What if I have to come live here?

I don't like my home, but I guess I'm used to it. Somehow

the idea of leaving, even separate from the idea of the fight that must lead up to it, made me uncomfortable. Also, I thought I didn't want to strain my friendship with Aunt Mil. I thought we could stand a good deal of pressure—I was pretty sure—but better not to test.

Pish was on the couch, a brilliant spot of color in the dark room. Aunt Mil actively likes brown, unlike some sad people who can see no other color. She chooses rich or spicy hues in a variety of textures, and usually I enjoy the effect. Some days, though, it's just brown.

The kitten pushed her front paws straight out in the extremist possible stretch and yawned, all teeth and slanting eyes. I scooped her up before she could flit. She struggled a little but purred, too, and I held her to my ear a second to hear the soothing vibrations. After all, I would rather have a cat.

Coming out the back door, I saw the scene at the table afresh. Aunt Mil sat straight-backed and high-headed, looking gravely at the dog. The greyhound lay nose on paws, and her troubled eyes gazed off at scenes I couldn't see.

As I came near she sat up, and her thin tail briefly stirred the grass. I put the struggling Pish into Aunt Mil's hands and took my dog by the collar. With a very severe expression Aunt Mil brought the kitten down to her level.

The greyhound stretched her nose forward to sniff. As nose touched fur, dog and kitten froze. I could feel the dog's great excitement, in the stiffness of her neck and the way her sniffing rocked her. She nudged the kitten in the stomach, and I couldn't tell if it was a motherly gesture or the preliminary nudge a canine gives its prey before the feast.

Pish was offended, and at a second nudge she tapped the greyhound's nose smartly, squirmed free, and scooted under the porch. The greyhound rose to her feet, hindquarters quivering.

Aunt Mil looked grim. "They let them chase and kill rabbits," she said, "training them to race."

"It's only natural for a dog to chase something that runs."

"I know. She'd need to be tied, or have a kennel." Already Aunt Mil was looking around the yard for a suitable spot, as if it were decided.

"Our house is really the best place for her," I said. "There's nothing she can hurt."

"Other than the family structure, no." Aunt Mil smiled one of her downturned, sour smiles. "Oh, Kris," she said, and cuffed her hard old hand lightly across the top of my head. "But she *is* lovely, and I'm sure she'll be a good dog to you."

"Oh, I forgot . . ." I told her about the little incident with Greg. She enjoyed that. She doesn't get along with Greg any better than she gets along with my father.

"But I can't keep calling her 'the dog.' Let's give her a name before I take her home."

We sat a long time there in the shade, drinking tea and looking at the dog, who looked back occasionally with that lurking smile. She politely refused all offers of gingersnaps.

"Sirius—because she's such a serious dog."

"Too serious for such a punning name."

"Beauty?"

Aunt Mil shook her head. "I know it's a name people give dogs, but I hate to hear it made so common."

We sat and thought some more. I was getting distracted. The coming fight was like far-off thunder in my mind, and the present, peaceful moment seemed quite temporary.

"Call her Diana," said Aunt Mil, after a long silence. "Diana the Huntress."

Diana, I repeated to myself, Diana. It is a classical name, though one forgets that. "Diana," I said, and probably because I spoke directly to her, looking straight into her face, the dog responded, flattening her ears and sweeping her tail through the grass.

"Okay. Diana."

She was panting, and it occurred to me as I took a sip of iced tea that she, too, must be thirsty. Though I'm always thinking about animals, I'm not used to being responsible for them yet.

I got her a bowl of water, which she drank, and then it was time to go. The dark August shadows were stretching long, and a cooling breeze stirred. Dad would be coming home, and I should be there before him.

"Do you want a ride?" asked Aunt Mil.

"No. You shouldn't be involved in this."

She smiled tartly. "I'll take you halfway."

Diana sat proud and fearful in the backseat of the VW and committed no transgressions. In the close confines of the car, she smelled distinctly doggy.

The distance was short by car, and in a very few minutes Aunt Mil pulled over to the curbside and switched off the engine. We sat silent, not willing to part. We were both fearful of impending change and tickled at the idea. I'd already made a mental list of things to bring and things to leave behind.

"I don't know why, but this seems like the time to tell you," Aunt Mil said abruptly. "That house is yours when I die."

I looked at her.

"Well, it has to happen, and the odds are it has to happen pretty soon. You know that, of course."

I try never to think about it, because it's so obviously true.

"Thought you should know," Aunt Mil said brusquely. "Ace up your sleeve, so to speak. Sell it to pay for your schooling—and that makes you independent, if you want to be." She looked out the side window and changed the subject.

"Try not to involve your mother any more than you can help."

"That'll be easy!"

She shrugged. "Well, Kris, you can't have it both ways. Just keep it between you and your father, all right? It could make things a good deal easier for me, later on."

"Okay." I got out of the car, and Diana followed as quickly as the seat was folded forward for her. "She doesn't think VWs are dignified," I told Aunt Mil. "If we come to live with you, you'll have to get a Mercedes."

Snort!

"I'd better not call you tonight," I said. "Unless I have to."

"No, I agree. Come early tomorrow, then. I'll be anxious."

We waved goodbye, and Diana and I went down the street together. I listened to the sound behind me of the old VW turning around in a driveway and going off in the opposite direction.

For a greyhound and a tall, athletic girl, we went very slowly. Diana paused to decorate the sidewalk, and I considered the responsibility I'd taken on; dog food and pooper scoopers, and training her not to chase cats. And what if she barked a lot?

But as if already trained to it, she walked at my side, never pulling. Her long, thin head looked strained and tired, split

Winning

by a nervous pant. She left a spotted trail of drips along the
sidewalk. I thought how little this whole thing had to do
with her. It was the family issue that was important. The
dog herself was a mere catalyst, and when it was over, she
would be my bonus. I hadn't taken her because I wanted a
dog. I'd taken her because I wanted at last to win.

Just like the racing people who sent her to be killed.

That seemed an indecent degree of power to hold over a
fellow creature—whole races of fellow creatures—pigs and
chickens and cows and horses, cats and rabbits and dogs and
goats. The power of use, of ownership, of disposal. I had
never seen it quite that way. I had never before owned an
animal.

In no conquering mood, solemn, disturbed, and uncertain,
I turned onto our street. A few seconds later a car turned
behind me and passed. I saw Amy's startled face at the window, and Mum's head turning sharply as the car veered
toward the Perellis' hedge.

I just kept walking. I was too tired, now, to nerve myself
for this engagement. It hadn't been a strenuous day by normal standards, yet I saw the street through a long gray tunnel. My eyes prickled and my limbs were heavy. I wanted
only to get to the kitchen and sit.

When I turned into our drive, Mum and Amy stood by the
car waiting; almost identical short, blond people, with
shocked china-blue eyes. Diana stopped walking when she
saw them.

"No, it's okay, girl. Come on." I gave the leash a gentle tug
and she came, with a brief, eloquent glance at my face.

"Kris," said Mum, "who does that dog belong to?"

"She belongs to me." I was walking past her into the

house, but just before she said, "Kristin!" in a most dangerous tone, I realized that this was both brazen and unfair.

I stopped and said, "She's a racing greyhound, and she was brought to be killed. Phillip saved her life."

Mum started to look a little pop-eyed.

"There were three others they did kill." My voice felt slow, furry, and stumbling. "They kill ten or twelve greyhounds a week there, Phillip says."

"Why didn't *he* keep her?" asked Mum, seizing on the most important point.

"He can't. They have so many expenses with his father—"

"Well, you can't, either, young lady, and you'd better figure something else to do with it before your father gets home."

I shook my head. "Amy, I have to go get her some dog food. If I tie her to the clothes pole, will you make sure she doesn't chew through the leash?"

Amy looked dazed with conflict. Most times she's solidly allied with Mum. She's an onlooker who doesn't get involved in these battles. Now she was staring at Diana, in deep fascination.

"Will she bite me, Kris?"

"No. Come pet her."

Amy came timidly, and stroked Diana's head. Her clean pink hand, which knew all about manicures and hairstyling, did not know how to pet a dog. Diana rolled a worried eye at me but allowed it.

"Wow! She's so *smooth*! Come feel her, Mum!"

Poor Mum. As soon as Amy left her side and the two of us started talking, she started to look helpless. At Amy's bidding she came to touch Diana, and her hand knew how. Perhaps a dog isn't so different from a kindergartner—and Mum didn't always live in my father's house. She comes from Aunt Mil's family, after all.

"I thought greyhounds were nervous," she murmured.

"She is. She just doesn't show it."

Mum's hand smoothed Diana's long skull. "She's very beautiful—"

An unspoken *but* hung in the air. Now was the time to move on, before it could be uttered. "Just watch her for fifteen minutes, Amy," I said, leading Diana through the breezeway to the backyard.

"Okay, but hurry up." Amy didn't want to be the one holding the dog when Dad got home.

"Be right back," I told Diana when she was securely tied. I pushed off on my bike, and strength came back to my legs as I pedaled down the street. It felt good to be going away, free and fast.

Tomorrow I'll get a dog-training book from the library and teach her to run alongside the bike. A greyhound could keep up.

When I got home, Dad still wasn't back. I opened a can of food and dumped it in an aluminum pie plate. When Diana had eaten it and then answered the call of nature, and when I had cleaned up the lawn with rake and shovel, I decided to bring her inside. Tied out back to the clothes pole, she looked as if she only half belonged. I didn't care to give Dad even that intangible advantage.

I untied her from the pole and led her up the cement steps, opened the door. She looked in uncertainly, ears flat, tail invisible between her legs. "Come on," I said. "It's okay."

She didn't think so, but when I tugged on the leash, she came creeping in, tail clamped up against her belly. I didn't like to see her fear, and I looked at Mum to check for sympathy.

But Mum was far away. She stood at the counter unwrapping a package of pork chops, with a tight, worried frown on her face.

I felt angry for a second, because no matter how unfair Dad is with me, he doesn't drag her into these fights. I don't become *her* child when I'm disgraced. It wasn't fair for her to look worried.

"Look," I said, "why don't you clear out? Take Amy shopping or something. No reason you should be mixed up in this."

Her eyes fixed on me and gradually became quite angry. "Thank you, Kris," she said, "I'll stay right here!" Her hands quickened, fixing the chops, and for a few minutes she looked very like Aunt Mil.

I found an old plastic container and filled it with water for Diana. She followed me to the sink, and back to my chair at the kitchen table. Only when she was sitting there tight beside me, politely refusing the water, did she betray any sign of knowing there was raw meat around. Her muzzle tilted up just slightly, and her long nose twitched. She licked her chops once. Then she sighed and stretched herself out beside the chair in a way that emphasized the hardness of the polished pine floor. She was the kind of dog, I thought, who would appreciate a soft bed of her own.

We waited. Mum made salad and biscuits. Amy showered and dried her hair. Once the phone rang. That was Greg, saying he wouldn't be home to supper. Mum folded her lips and wrapped two of the chops to put back in the refrigerator. Opening the door, she glanced briefly at Diana.

"Phillip says they feed them rotten raw meat," I said. "They all have worms."

"Well, these aren't rotten, and she's not getting them!" Mum put the chops away but lingered a moment at the refrigerator door. "She'll need a worm pill, I suppose. And vaccinations . . ."

"I have money for all that stuff."

"Of course you do," said Mum impatiently. "Money is the *last* thing at issue here. But Kris . . ." She glanced at the clock, and then back at me, squarely. It was the first time in ages I could remember her looking at me without thinking of something else.

"Kris . . ." she said, and hesitated again, embroiled in a difficult thought. At last her eyes refocused, and she burst out, "He ought to be proud of you! The two of you are just exactly alike, and maybe if you give him a chance, he'll see that."

"*Me* give *him* a chance?"

"Somebody has to start it, and if you wait for him, you'll wait a good long time!"

"He's the adult," I said. It sounded thin—I'm always thinking I'm more adult than he is, after all. But the man has twenty-five years on me! It seems reasonable to expect a higher level of maturity.

Mum might have gone into all this, but just then we heard a car turn into the driveway and pause there, engine running. Dad said goodbye to someone in a cheerful voice. There was a moment while the bag of clubs was maneuvered out of the backseat, and then the car door closed with a hearty thunk and Dad was coming up the steps. Mum's face masked over. She put the chops on the broiling rack.

THE SIXTH SENSE

Through the screen door I saw him in his bright lime-green golf shirt, his face fresh with sun and exercise, and a happy, victorious set to his shoulders. His eyes were unguarded, his lips half open with glad tidings. The door latch rattled. Diana swallowed, making a sticky sound with her tongue, and sat up as he came through the door. He stopped halfway and stood looking at her.

For the first several seconds he was merely stunned. Slowly his eyes grew as cold as two stones. He raised them to look at me.

Dad's eyes must always be met. That's the first line of defense, before words, and sometimes instead of words. Sometimes this is hard, and other times I'm able to be limpid and innocent, which infuriates him. Now I was too tired for either. My eyes were only seeing, not making any statements. It didn't seem to be what he'd expected.

"Kristin, what is going on here?"

"The racing people brought four greyhounds to the vet to be killed," I said. "Phillip saved this one, and since he can't keep a dog, I took her."

Dad's gaze dropped to Diana, and the frown deepened. He looked not furious but unhappy. Slowly he came through the door, bumping it with the bag of clubs and not closing it.

"Damn it, Kris," he said, and swept past us, upstairs to put the clubs away.

I'd thought I was ready for him, but I wasn't ready for this. I'd never expected to feel guilty, or sorry for him. I looked to Mum, who was softly closing the door, but her face was turned away.

Diana pressed against my leg and I stroked her neck, remembering; she has the most to lose.

The golf clubs thumped down in their corner, and Dad's

174

steps quickened, down the hall and down the stairs, as elastic as Greg's in his soft-soled sport shoes. He's gotten himself angry now, I thought, and was relieved.

He came around the corner and said, "Call the Humane Society, Kris. They'll come get it."

Here was the moment for my simple act of defiance. A one-word answer was all that was required. But even as I drew in the long breath needed for that word, Mum was interrupting.

"Steve, they don't pick animals up! You have to go to them."

"All right," said Dad, taking the keys from the counter.

"Steve, *supper*," breathed Mum.

Dad looked baffled and irritated. "Right after then," he said.

"You can't do that," I said. "She's my dog."

"And I have told you—*innumerable* times—that I will not allow pets in this house."

"Why not?"

"Because it's a waste and a nuisance! A waste of money, a waste of time, and a waste of emotional energy that might be better spent on your own family!"

"Why is it any worse than soccer or golf?"

That balked him for a minute. He glared at me, waiting for a good answer to occur to him.

"Sport," he said at last, "is a time-honored human activity—"

"Keeping animals is a heck of a lot older than playing golf," I said, bouncing into the middle of his uncompleted thought. But a triumphant smile lit his eyes, and I knew I'd somehow left an opening.

"Keeping *animals* is older, yes," he said. "I've no objection

to keeping animals for utilitarian purposes, as you can see."
He gestured to the platter of pork chops that Mum was placing on the table. "But the keeping of *pets* I regard as a degradation of the older impulse—and, I might add, a degradation
of the animal. Think of all the years of human-controlled
breeding that brought a wild, self-sufficient animal to *that*
state!" He gestured at Diana, who stood pressed to my leg,
her eyes dark with suffering and bewilderment.

It was my turn to fix my opponent with a glare while I
groped for an answer. In the periphery of my vision I was
aware of Mum bringing the salad and biscuits to the table.
She went away, and I heard her at the stairs, calling Amy to
supper.

I remembered at last an argument. "But they're *here*!" I
said. "Maybe it is degradation, but that's the way things
are!"

"I choose not to participate," said Dad rather grandly.
Mum speared a pork chop and put it on his plate. Absently
and automatically he sat in his chair, never taking his eyes
from me—as one dog eats in the presence of another, never
letting down its guard.

"This dog doesn't have that choice," I said. "She *had* to
participate—in good old time-honored sport! And she wasn't
good enough, so they could snuff her out anytime they
wanted. I think that's . . ." I searched for a word strong
enough. Dad took it from the tip of my tongue.

"Obscene." His eyes dropped at last to his plate. He took
up knife and fork to cut his pork chop. But when he had a
piece separated, he put down the silverware again, reaching
for the glass of wine Mum had poured him and looking at
Diana.

"Once there was a reason for a dog like that," he said.

"They caught game for people—food for the table. Now they're just . . . an amusement for the decadent. A way to get something for nothing, if you're lucky. Should be abolished."

"But she's *here!*" I said. "She's alive! That's reason enough—" Bang! A kick landed on my shin, and I broke off to look in amazement at Amy, placidly eating beside me.

Before I could figure it out, Dad was saying, "Yes, she's here, but she's not staying! I agree that the situation is deplorable—but I do not want a dog!"

"It doesn't matter what you want," I said. "She's—ow! Amy, why are you kicking me?"

"Steven, another pork chop?" Mum asked as Dad glared at Amy and me speechlessly.

"I haven't even started this one! Kris, she goes—and if we can't have a civilized meal here, then she goes this minute!"

"If she goes, I go."

It would have been nice to be steady and cool about it, but my voice was a little wild, a little wobbly. Dad looked at me with some of the fire dying out of his eyes. When he spoke again, it was in a quieter voice.

"What does your Aunt Mil have to do with all this?"

"Nothing!"

"But you'll go to her, won't you?"

I didn't want to answer, but he didn't press it. He looked down at his plate again and ate the piece of pork chop he had cut off many minutes ago. He chewed a long time, as if it were tough, and laid down his fork again.

"Kris, this is exactly the sort of sentimental gesture I despise. No dog is worth the breakup of a family—and this is a dog you can't even . . ." He hesitated over the word, but at last got himself to pronounce it. "This is a dog you can't even *love* yet. You've only had it a few hours."

I looked at Diana, by my knee. No, I certainly didn't love her, as kids in books love their dogs. I didn't even love her as much as I loved Robert or Pish. But that didn't matter.

"She still has a right to live," I said, "and I have a right to keep her."

I thought he'd jump me on that one, but he didn't. He's never quite as blatant about being the sole authority in the home as Aunt Mil and I make him out to be. Perhaps he truly believes our family is a democracy.

I was still waiting for the fight to begin in earnest; the force might be overwhelming, but I braced against it, with the thought of Aunt Mil like a pistol in my pocket. Soon I would have to whip it out. Soon my back would be against the wall and I would have no choice.

Dad went back to his chop. The frown lightened on his brow until it was only a shallow line. He sipped his wine quietly and said nothing.

Okay, he's waiting until after supper. Then we'll start the Humane Society bit again.

I ate, too, and Diana eased herself down on the floor beside my chair. Natural dignity did for her what training did for other dogs. In a room resounding with herself as an issue, she, as creature, was completely unobtrusive.

Dessert was ice cream, and coffee for Mum and Dad. He remembered his golf game and told her about it. His eyes, having withdrawn, never once returned to me while I was watching.

At last he stood, cup in hand, and went to the counter, where Diana's borrowed leash and the car keys lay next to the coffee maker. He poured himself another cup, not seeming to notice anything else, picked up the newspaper, and retired to his living-room chair.

I gaped after him in complete astonishment, and then I started to get mad. I *hate* being ignored! I got up from the table, stepping over Diana to go after him. But she sat up at the wrong moment, and as I clothespinned her between my legs and nearly fell, Mum said, "Kris!"

Her voice was deadly quiet, the voice that made me, as a little child, do what I didn't want. "Kris," she said, "get out of here."

I opened my mouth to argue. She shook her head. "Don't push," she said. "Don't push."

All at once I felt close to tears. Not looking at anyone, I snapped the leash on Diana's collar and we went out. Down the walk and down the quiet street, now in purple twilight.

I felt crushed. I'd won. It seemed like I had won, but nothing was solved and nothing was changed. I didn't want it to be that easy.

I remembered the kitten I wanted when I was ten—a beautiful, fluffy, black-and-white kitten. Now it seemed like I could have had him, if I'd just tried harder. I could have cried right there on the open sidewalk, wanting that kitten all over again.

Diana watered the Perellis' hedge and then came along easily, claws clicking on the asphalt. I spoke her name, and she glanced up with flattened ears and her secretly smiling eyes.

Okay, one thing has changed. I have Diana.

I have Diana, and I won. But I didn't change his mind. I just outmuscled him. I scared him, and he backed down. I never would have thought he'd do that.

And it wasn't good enough. It was a bullying way to win— the way he'd always won, by strategic position, not strength of argument. I wanted to *convince* him.

"She has a right to live!" I shouted at him inside. "I have a right to keep her! You can't keep denying me—I have somewhere else to go! I have somewhere else to go!"

"Go, then," he said inside me.

But he didn't say that. I almost ripped the family structure apart, and he would not allow it. "No dog is worth the breakup of a family," he said, and he meant it. He really meant it, because he let me defeat him.

Oh, God! I sat down on a fire hydrant and pressed my fingers to my eyes. I don't understand . . .

Gently the loop of the leash moved on my wrist as Diana ranged. Sniffing sounds—she seemed to pick something up, and then she stood very still.

"She doesn't even know how to play," said Phillip. I opened my eyes. He was standing there before her. She had a dusty old red sock in her mouth. Her eyes were merry and uncertain, her tail waving low. Phillip made a gentle snatch for the sock. Diana averted her head, looking unhappy.

He caught the sock and tugged softly. Almost without meaning to, it seemed, Diana tugged back. Her eyes started to smile again; her tail waved gently. Maybe this was funny?

"You can keep her?" Phillip asked, pulling harder on the sock. Diana braced. Her tail sank again.

"Yes," I said. I must have sounded more defeated than anything else. Phillip delicately skirted that, not noticing, not ignoring.

"Then let's take her up to the athletic field," he said, "and teach her how to play."